Broken
Crayons
and
Sand
in
their
Shoes

Broken Crayons and Sand in their Shoes

written by

Lloyd Wright

iUniverse
New York Bloomington

BROKEN CRAYONS AND SAND IN THEIR SHOES

Copyright © 2009 by Lloyd Wright

iUniverse books may be ordered through booksellers or by contacting:

iUniverse
1663 Liberty Drive
Bloomington, IN 47403
www.iuniverse.com
1-800-Authors (1-800-288-4677)

Because of the dynamic nature of the Internet, any Web addresses or links contained in this book may have changed since publication and may no longer be valid. This is a work of fiction. All of the characters, names, incidents, organizations, and dialogue in this novel are either the products of the author's imagination or are used fictitiously.

ISBN: 978-1-4401-2331-3 (pbk)
ISBN: 978-1-4401-2333-7 (hbk)
ISBN: 978-1-4401-2332-0 (ebk)

Printed in the United States of America
iUniverse rev. date: 3/10/09

OTHER BOOKS IN PRINT
By Lloyd Wright

"BACK THEN UNTIL NOW" (Poems)
ISBN: 0-595-34975-7 (Paperback)
ISBN: 0-595-67180-2 (Hardcover)

"POEMS AND THOUGHTS"
ISBN: 0-595-31234 (Paperback)
ISBN: 0-595-66281 (Hardcover)

"GRAMP'S CHRISTMAS TALES"
ISBN: 0-595-41162-7 (Paperback)
ISBN: 0-595-85520-2 (Hardcover)

"STORIES FOR GRAMPS LITTLE FRIENDS"
ISBN: 0-595-31266-7 (Paperback)
ISBN: 0-595-66287-0 (Hardcover)

"MORE STORIES FOR GRAMPS LITTLE FRIENDS"
ISBN: 0-595-33310-9 (Paperback)
ISBN: 0-595-66836-4 (Hardcover)

"GRAMPS SHORT STORIES AND TALL TALES"
ISBN-13: 978-0-595-37755-8 (paperback)
ISBN-13: 978-0-595-67561 (hardback)
ISBN-13: 978-0-595-82130-3 (ebk)
ISBN-10: 0-595-37755-6 (paperback)
ISBN-10: 0-595-67561-1 (hardcover)
ISBN-10: 0-595-82130-8 (ebk)

"DONNA, DONNIE AND LITTLE SAD WEE WILLY"
ISBN:978-14257-5387-0 (softcover)

"GRAMP'S VARIETY OF STORIES"
ISBN: 978-595-47731-9 (softcopy)
ISBN : 978-595-71311-0 (hardcover)
ISBN: 978-595-91994-9(EBK)
All books can be ordered at all major bookstores or online at:
www.iuniverse.com
www.barnesandnoble.com
www.amazon.com
www.booksamillion.com
www.xlibris.com

e-mail: lmwright@arkansas.net

DEDICATION

This book is dedicated to all the past and present kindergarten friends I have read to and to their teachers.

FRONT COVER

The picture on the front cover is of my Great Grandson Garrett Gentry and his friend Elizabeth Sprouse emptying sand out of their shoes and holding a broken crayon.

BACK COVER

The young lady on the back cover with me is one of my friends I read to when she was in kindergarten. The story titled, "Maddie", is about this young lady.

SPECIAL ACKNOWLEDGMENT

I wish to thank Daniel, Heather and Maddie Gomer for allowing me to include the story, "Maddie," in the book.

SPECIAL RECOGNITION

Jan and Wayne Fuller have helped me tremendously in the publication of this book. Jan proof read while Wayne gave me encouragement and set up the book. You two are very special friends.

About the Book

"Broken Crayons and Sand in their Shoes," is a book containing twenty one short stories and one poem. The title of the book and the stories which contain reference to broken crayons and sand in their shoes are from observing the children I read to. When they come in from the playground their shoes are full of sand and broken crayons are lying on the floor.

Since Christmas is my favorite time of the year several stories are about Christmas. Other stories are about animals and children. The story Maddie, was written to make people aware of diabetes. It used to be uncommon for children to have diabetes but not any more. I tried to incorporate in my book stories showing love, laughter, sharing, and giving.

I am a volunteer that is lucky enough to find kindergarten classes that will share their time with me. They all call me, "Gramps."

Contents

SAND IN THEIR SHOES

GRAMPS was waiting in a kindergarten classroom for the students to come in from the playground. He had seen them lining up to come in from the playground when he arrived to read to the class as a volunteer. Before too long he heard the sound of their little voices in the hallway. They were supposed to have, "quiet time," in the hall; but how could children in their first week of kindergarten keep quiet?

Gramps did not have to wait long before sweaty little boys and girls traipsed into the classroom. After some encouragement from their teacher, the students found their desk and were fidgeting in their seats. When they all were seated, then they were allowed to get a much needed drink, by rows, to quench their thirst. Gramps requested the boys in each row let the girls go first as that was the gentlemanly thing to do. Some boys responded by letting the girls go first while others did not. Oh well, politeness takes time and maybe before the end of the month they would let the girls go first even though they did not let their sisters go first at home.

After all the students had quenched their thirst and were seated at their desk, the teacher introduced Gramps to her new kindergarten class. Gramps soon found out the children were more interested in the sand in their shoes from the playground than they were to meet him.

He was not surprised since this would be a daily occurrence as he had learned from previous years. He once questioned.

"How can there be any sand left on the playground judging from the amount they carry into the classroom in their shoes?"

The students who had sand in their shoes were allowed to go two at a time to empty the sands out of their shoes and into the trash can by the teacher's desk. Gramps took this opportunity to help those who could not tie their shoes laces and to visit with them. During this time he found out some very important information. One student informed him that part of his shoes lace was missing because his dog had chewed on it. This caused another student to inform Gramps his dog was missing part of his ear; he thought the neighbor's cat ate it. One little girl then informed Gramps her doll had short hair since she had given it a hair cut with her new scissors her mom had bought her for school. Another young lad told this tale as he sat on the floor emptying sand out of his shoes.

"I don't need help tying my shoes because my momma bought me shoes with Velcro because I don't know how to tie shoes. She had my cat de-clawed and now we have piles in the yard because my cat can't dig a hole. My mom told me to watch where I walk in the grass. You know cat stuff smells bad."

As Gramps continued helping tie shoe laces after the students emptied the sand out of their shoes, his knowledge increased as each student had to have their little chit chat. One young man told Gramps.

"I told my mom not to cry when she brought me to the room or it would make me cry and that would embarrass me."

A little blue eyed girl informed Gramps that her dog and cat missed her and did not want her to go to school because they had to stay outside in the yard while she was gone. Another boy had to show

Gramps the holes in his socks. He went on to say.

"My mom said no one would see the holes in my socks since they were inside of my shoes."

As a little brown eyed sad faced girl pulled off her shoes and emptied the sand out she told Gramps.

"My cat Lucille climbed on the screen door and tore a hole in it. My Dad said he hoped the cat would run away; my cat is gone now so I guess it did."

When her friend heard her story, she had to tell Gramps her dog just died; she don't know why, it just did. Gramps continued helping the children with their shoes as they removed the playground sand from them. Then he heard a story he wish he had just listened and not asked a question. A little dark eyed boy with a smile as big as the world told Gramps.

"My dog Duke has to stay outside all the time."

Well Gramps just had to ask.

"Why?"

The little boy with the huge smile answered.

"Because he pooties all the time and slides his behind on the carpet."

Gramps got his question answered. Won't he ever learn?

Gramps watched as a shy young man took off his shoes and emptied sand in the trash can. He could tell he had something very important to say. As Gramps tied his shoes, the young man whispered to Gramps.

"My Grandma hates my dog because he digs in her flowers and rolls in the dirt and Grandpa hates my cat because it never covers up what it does in the yard. Grandpa said he knows the cat does it so he can watch him step in it when he mows the grass."

While Gramps was busy tying one young man's shoes, a little girl was patiently waiting for him to get done so he could fix her broken crayon. When she showed it to him and asked him to fix it, he told her it could not be fixed. Little tears filled her eyes as she said.

"My mom told me she would spank me if I did not take good care of my colors. She said she would not buy anymore."

Gramps took the crayon and put it back together with scotch tape. He told her.

"When you see the first star tonight make a wish for a little fairy to buy you some new crayons."

When Gramps finished reading to the class that day, he stopped at a local store and bought a new box of crayons. While the students were getting on the bus to go home, a little fairy was in a certain kindergarten room replacing a used box of crayons with a new box. As the fairy looked around the room, he smiled when he saw broken crayons lying on a sandy floor. If the janitors did not clean the room daily, the students would have enough sand from their shoes in a week's time to build a sand castle under a broken crayon rainbow. Broken crayons and sand in their shoes had given Gramps a great day and a content smile on his face. He had learned a lot about children, pets, etc.

MOLLY

LITTLE Kyle Wyatt leaned against the kitchen table as he ate a hot oatmeal cookie. His mother could tell he had something on his mind he wanted to discuss with her. He is an energetic boy and always up to something. The fact he had been crippled by polio did not slow him down. His dad had made him a pair of crutches to assist him to venture around the farm. Kyle had just had his eighth birthday, when polio had found him and left him with a crippled left leg. As his mother looked into his sparkling blue eyes, he asked her.

"Can I have a Shetland pony? I could ride it to school next month when school starts. Dad said I can't walk that far and he would have to take me to school everyday. I would take good care of it."

She gave him another oatmeal cookie and then said.

"Go talk to your father."

Kyle took but just a second to eat the warm oatmeal cookie and then hobbled outside with his crutches. He had heard his dad working in the barn earlier so that is where he went first. It was just about time to milk the cows anyway. He helped his dad with the chore of milking and had since he was six years old. The cow he milked was a small cow and went by the name of Abby. Kyle would feed her extra hay when his dad wasn't looking. Abby was his friend and would follow him when he walked in the pasture. Kyle opened the barn door and found his dad putting grain in the manger along with some hay for the cows to eat when they were in the barn to be milked.

Kyle hobbled over to a bale of hay and sat down. As he sat there watching his dad put feed in the manger, he felt a cold nose push under his hand. It was Fetch, the dog, trying to get some attention. He had followed Kyle to the barn. Kyle knew the reason his dad called the dog Fetch was because when Fetch was a puppy he would fetch anything his dad threw and told him to fetch. He even goes into the pasture and fetches the cows when his dad tells him to. When his dad finished putting the feed in the manger, he came over and sat on the bale of hay with his son. As he put his arm around him he asked.

"What brings you out here? It is too early to get the cows in the barn to milk."

Kyle leaned against his dad and replied.

"I asked mom if I could have a Shetland pony to ride to school when school starts again since I can't walk to school. It is about two miles and you wouldn't have to take me to school everyday. She told me to ask you."

His dad gave him a gentle hug as he replied.

"Son, I would love to get you a pony but the very truth is a pony cost a lot of money and we don't have any extra money for a pony. I know you don't understand but someday you will."

When Kyle was milking Abby later that afternoon, he kept up a steady conversation with her. He told Abby.

"You know if you were a pony I could ride you to school. I like it when Dad puts me on your back and you give me a ride around the barnyard. I don't think you would like the long walk to school. My friends would like to see you. You know my friend Elsie has a pony but she can't ride it anymore. She is sick with polio and is in a cast from the waist down. I feel so sorry for her. She let me ride on her pony when she was well. My friend Bobby has polio and is in an iron lung. You know Abby, I am lucky, I may be crippled but I can still go outside; Elsie and Bobby can't. Dad has given me a ride on Smokey and Sandy but they are big horses and I couldn't ride them to school. They are too big and I couldn't get up on their back by myself anyway; besides Dad needs them to help him work in the fields."

Kyle's dad listened as his son kept up a steady chatter to the cow he was milking. He knew Kyle was having a hard time milking Abby but he sure had spunk and wanted to help his dad. He wished there was a way he could get Kyle a pony. It would take a miracle for him to find enough money to buy a pony when they were now just barely getting by on the sparse money they were so fortunate to have. He knew a pony would give him more time to do the farm work and going to school in the morning and afternoon would sure take a chunk out of his work time.

Before Kyle crawled into his bed that night, he folded his hands and knelt as best as his crippled leg would let him. He bowed his head and said.

"I sure would like to have a Shetland pony to ride to school. It would help my Dad and I would take good care of it. I don't care what color it is or if it is a boy or girl pony. I wouldn't even need a saddle and it would be my friend just like Abby and Fetch. I wouldn't need a pony if my leg wasn't crippled but the doctor don't know if I will ever be able to walk without the crutches my dad made for me. Would you help my mom and dad? Sometimes I see my mom cry because I am crippled and she can't help me like she wants to. Thank you for Fetch; he helps me a lot and lets me lean on him and helps me walk without one of my crutches. Amen."

After Kyle had said his prayers and was tucked in bed for the night, his parents sat on the front porch and listened to the night sounds. It was always a peaceful time of day for them. They quietly discussed Kyle's wish for a pony but both agreed it would be impossible to buy him one. They would be lucky to have enough money to get through the winter and have enough left to buy seeds for spring planting. They discussed how polio had struck Kyle and two of his classmates during the last school year. They agreed they were lucky he had a milder case of polio. His little friend Elsie is in a cast and may never walk again. Elsie and her parents live just down the road a half mile toward the school. They are such nice neighbors. The sound of the porch swing fit right in with the sounds of night as they gently swung with his brawny arm around her as she lay with her head against his chest. It was so quiet she could hear his heart beat above the chirp of the crickets. She looked up and said to her husband.

"Jim everything has a special way of working out."

She then reached up and gave him a little kiss.

Kyle awoke the next morning to the sound of his mother in the kitchen and his dad carrying the milk pails to the barn as they clanged together. Just as he was getting out of the warm bed, his mother gently called for him to get up; it was time for him to help his dad milk the cows before breakfast. Kyle crawled into his overall and put on a shirt. His dad always milked the cows while his mom prepared breakfast. He had told Kyle.

"Breakfast taste better if you have done a little work first."

Breakfast always tasted good to Kyle after he had milked Abby; yes, his dad was right. Sometimes they could smell the bacon frying when they were coming toward the house with full milk buckets. Kyle hobbled out to the barn with his crutches and received a friendly welcome.

"Good morning Son." His dad said.

Then he received a lick on the hand from Fetch and a friendly, moo, from Abby. The sun was just peeking over the horizon. Kyle just knew this was going to be a great day!

After the milking was through, they turned the cows out into the pasture for the day and separated the morning milking. They both washed their hands when they were through and ready for breakfast. Kyle's mom had breakfast ready and sitting on the table. She had fried some of the eggs Kyle had gathered from the hen house the evening before. That was one of his daily chores. It was hard carrying the eggs with his crutches so Fetch always helped him. Fetch would gently carry the egg basket in his mouth. Kyle's dad said Grace and then it was time to eat. During breakfast Kyle wanted to ask just one more time for a pony but knew better. His dad said.

"Kyle, you better eat a hearty breakfast because today you and I have to clean the stalls in the barn and haul what we clean out to the fields and spread it with the manure spreader."

After breakfast, Kyle hobbled out to the barn with his crutches and watched as his dad put the harness on the team of horses. When he had Smokey and Sandy harnessed, he picked Kyle up and placed him on Smokey's back. Kyle hung onto the harness hames as his dad led the horses out of the barn and over to hitch them to the manure spreader. After the team was hitched to the manure spreader, Kyle's dad took him off of Smokey's back and sat him on the seat of the spreader. Then off toward the barn they went to clean out the stalls.

Kyle and his dad were in the barn cleaning out the stalls when Elsie's dad, Mr. Tucker came in the barn door. Kyle saw him first and said.

"Hi Mr. Tucker, Dad and I are cleaning out the stalls."

Mr. Tucker gave Kyle a huge smile as he picked him up and gave him a hug. After he sat Kyle down, Kyle's dad shook Mr. Tucker's hand and asked him.

"What brings you over here this time of morning?"

Mr. Tucker asked Jim, Kyle's dad, if they could talk outside. After they were outside Mr. Tucker said.

"Jim, I came over to see if you would do something for me. I wanted to keep Molly, Elsie's little pony but she is going blind. The Veterinarian told me she will not get any better and needs to be put down. He offered to put her to sleep but I am so short of money; I told him I would do it myself. I tried to put her down yesterday but I just couldn't do it. I came over this morning to see if you would put her down for me."

Kyle had been standing inside the barn listening to his dad and Mr. Tucker talk. When he heard what they were talking about, he hobbled as fast as he could out of the barn as he yelled.

"Let me have Molly. I will take good care of her. She can give me a ride to school even if she can't see. I will show her where to go and take good care of her until Elsie gets well. Please."

Both men were startled and had hoped Kyle would not hear their conversation. Finally Mr. Tucker said.

"Jim, I don't know. I would feel horrible if Kyle got hurt riding a pony who is going blind. I would give Molly to Kyle if you thought it could possible work out."

Kyle's dad thought a moment then replied.

"Let me talk to Mrs. Wyatt tonight about this. It just may not hurt a thing to give Kyle's suggestion a try. I will be over in the morning and give you an answer."

Mr. Tucker gave Kyle a pat on top of his head as he said.

"Kyle, I hate that Molly is going blind. She is such a young and gentle pony. If your parents decide you can have her, you be very careful when you ride her, with her losing her sight she will tend to stumble."

Mr. Tucker shook Kyle's dad hand as he said.

"Jim, I will see you in the morning. I won't keep you from your task of cleaning out the stall. I know Kyle just can't wait to get back in the barn and get his hands on a pitch fork."

He winked and grinned as he was talking. Fetch had been sitting by Kyle wagging his tail and listening as if he understood everything being said. When Mr. Tucker turned to leave, Fetch went over by him to get his usual pat on his head good-by. He liked Mr. Tucker, ever since he had met him when Kyle had gone to visit Elsie the first time and she let Kyle ride on Molly. Fetch and Molly had become good friends during this time also.

Kyle tried to sit on the porch swing with his parents after they had eaten supper and all the chores were done. He sat on the porch swing with them but just could not stay awake. The work he had done with his dad all day just helped make the sandman come early. He had wanted to stay awake to listen to his parents discuss Molly. After Kyle had fallen to sleep his dad carried him into the house and tucked him into bed. He returned to the swing on the porch and started the evening ritual of listening to the sounds of the evening with his wife tucked safely in his arm.

After they had settled in for the evening on the swing, he told her of his conversation with Mr. Tucker. She had already heard the whole story from Kyle and had been in deep thought arguing with her self over what to do while Jim had carried Kyle to bed. Fetch was dozing next to the swing but still listening for anything unusual going on in the darkness. Kyle's mom felt sorry for Molly and in the back of her mind she thought if Molly still has some eye sight left maybe she needed a chance at life. Her husband argued that Kyle could be injured riding a pony losing its eyesight. He also realized all the feed the pony would eat he could feed a milk cow and sell its milk. He kept thinking about the time it would cost him carrying Kyle to and from school when he needed to be working in the field. They both quietly discussed their feelings late into the night. They decided to get a good night's sleep and make their decision in the morning.

Kyle awoke the next morning before the rooster had crowed to welcome the new day. As he was slipping into his overalls, he heard his parents talking about Molly and then his dad going out of the door with the milk pails clanging together as he carried them. He hurriedly put on his shirt along with his socks and shoes. He didn't even tie his shoes before he headed for the kitchen. His mom was starting breakfast. When he stepped into the kitchen, he was met with her gentle smile as she told him.

"Your dad has already gone to the barn to milk the cows. You better run along and help him."

Kyle started to ask her about Mollie but instead put on his hat and out the door he hobbled with his crutches to help his dad.

As Kyle hobbled into the barn, he was met with a friendly.

"Good morning son; you better grab your milk pail and get Abby milked. After breakfast we need to go see if Mr. Tucker will still let you have Molly or if he has changed his mind."

Kyle could not believe what he had just heard. He stammered.

"Do I really get to have Molly?"

Kyle's dad replied.

"Your mother and I decided to see if it would work out okay. Your mom thinks Molly needs a chance as long as she still isn't completely blind. You will be completely responsible for Mollie's care."

Kyle picked up his milk pail and as he milked Abby, he kept up a continuous chatter with her about Molly.

After the milking was completed and the cows turned out into the pasture for the day, Kyle turned the handle on the milk separator for his dad and then helped him finish the morning chores before going in the house to eat breakfast. As they did the chores, Kyle became overly anxious to get the morning chores done so they could go get Molly. His dad cautioned him to feed all the animals as they should be fed and don't waste grain because he is in a rush. He said.

"Kyle, always remember to treat your animals with kindness; feed and water them properly. You know we depend on them to put food on our table and they must depend on us to feed and treat them right."

After all chickens, ducks, pigs, cows, and horses had been fed and watered, Kyle and his dad went into the house for a hot waiting breakfast. As they sat at the breakfast table, Kyle's parent's told him they were willing to take a chance and let him have Molly. He must be very careful when he rode her and the care would be up to him. They could not afford a saddle so he would have to ride Molly bareback. Kyle promised to take very, very, very good care of Molly and he didn't care if he had a saddle for her, just as long as he had a pony to ride to school and to take care of. Kyle's parents again cautioned him they were willing to give Molly a chance but if it didn't work out or proved to be too dangerous, then she would have to go to pony heaven.

After breakfast was finished, Kyle gave his mother a kiss and thanked her for giving Molly a chance and for letting him have her. Kyle's dad hugged his wife as he said.

"Mrs. Wyatt, you sure feed your family good. Kyle and I are going to ride Smokey over to see the Tuckers. If Mr. Tucker still agrees to give Kyle Molly, Kyle can ride her home."

Kyle already had hobbled out the kitchen door with his crutches and was anxiously waiting at the front yard gate with Fetch. Kyle's dad yelled to Kyle from the front porch.

"Your mother has some table scraps for Fetch; you know he needs to eat also. Why don't you feed him while I go out to the barn and put the bridle on Smokey so we can ride him over to the Tuckers?"

By the time Kyle's dad was leading Smokey out of the barn, Kyle had fed Fetch the table scraps and Fetch has already wolfed them down. Fetch then looked around to see if another dog had eaten his food since it had disappeared so fast from his dog dish. Kyle watched as his dad swung upon Smokey's back and rode to where he was standing. One of his dad's strong arms reached down and swept Kyle up into the air and deposited him on Smokey's back behind him. As Smokey plodded out of the driveway and turned up the dusty country road toward the Tuckers with an excited young lad, Fetch ran along side of them.

When Smokey turned into the Tucker's driveway, Mr. Tucker was just coming out of the barn. Kyle heard a little voice say, hi Mr. Wyatt.

He glanced over toward the house and saw little Ellie, Elsie's younger sister on the front porch watching. Kyle waved to Ellie and she wrinkled up her nose at him and then smiled. Little Ellie liked Kyle. He always talked to her when he had come over to visit her sister. Kyle and his dad rode on over by the barn. Kyle's dad lifted a leg over Smokey's neck and jump off. He shook Mr. Tucker's hand as he said.

"We came over to talk to you about Molly. Mrs. Wyatt and I would like to give Kyle a chance with Molly before she is totally blind and you put her down."

Mr. Tucker had been listening to Mr. Wyatt while he watched Fetch greet Molly in the lot next to the barn. Fetch and Molly were standing nose to nose. They had become friends when Kyle and Elsie had taken turns riding Molly. Kyle and the two men watched as Fetch wagged his tail and then ran a quick trip around Molly. Molly snorted and threw her head up in the air. Mr. Wyatt was surprised to see the two animals act like they were happy to be together again. Mr. Tucker said.

"Kyle, I have a bill of sale here in my pocket. I will need to have you and your dad sign it. It will make Molly legally yours and relieve me of any responsibility if you get hurt riding her. Kyle, you do realize she is nearly blind and soon won't be able to see at all."

Kyle shook his head yes, as he said.

"I will still take care of her even if she can't see."

Mr. Tucker replied.

"Kyle, I have written on the bill of sale that you agree to pay ten cents for her."

Kyle was startled. He was still sitting on Smokey's back. He said.

"Mr. Tucker, I don't have ten cents."

Mr. Tucker winked at Mr. Wyatt as he said.

"Jim, I think I see something in your boy's ear."

He reached up and felt Kyle's left ear. When he pulled his hand away, in the palm of his hand was a dime. He said.

"Kyle, as soon as you and your dad sign the bill of sale Molly is yours."

Mr. Wyatt reached up and lifted Kyle off of Smokey's back. Kyle held onto a panel gate so he wouldn't fall down. His crutches were still by the front yard gate where he had left them when his dad had lifted him up onto Smokey's back. After the bill of sale was signed, Kyle and his dad shook Mr. Tucker's hand and thanked him. Mr. Tucker then picked Kyle up and carried him into the barn lot and over to Molly. As he sat Kyle on Molly's back he said.

"Molly, meet your new owner and friend. He has given you a new lease on life."

Mr. Tucker then led Molly over to the barn and took off the halter and put Molly's bridle on her. He slid Kyle back onto Molly's hind quarters. He took a small saddle and placed it on Molly. Kyle was surprised and said.

"I don't have any money to buy the saddle; my dad told me I would have to ride her bareback."

Mr. Tucker smiled as he patted Kyle on his leg and replied.

"Kyle, this saddle isn't much and besides it is part of the deal. It was all I could afford for Elsie to use. If you keep it oiled and take care of it, it will last you a long time."

After he had tightened the girth strap, he lifted Kyle into the saddle and said.

"Jim, let's go up to the house and have a cup of coffee. Elsie wants to see Kyle."

He handed the reins to Kyle and then led Molly up to the front yard gate with Fetch following close behind. Mr. Tucker carried Kyle into the house and into the front room where Elsie was lying in bed. Mr. Tucker and Mr. Wyatt had a nice visit over a hot cup of coffee as there children talked in the front room. Ellie had followed her dad into the house and into the front room. She just had to hear what Kyle and her sister talked about.

When Kyle had told Elsie good-by, Ellie put her hands on her hips and said.

"Kyle, you had better take good care of my sister's pony!"

Kyle gave her a smile as he was carried out of the house by his dad. Fetch was standing by Molly at the front gate patiently waiting. Kyle was soon in the saddle and watched as his dad shook Mr. Tucker's hand and then mounted Smokey. Kyle told Mr. Tucker good-by and thank you and then told Molly.

"Giddy up."

He was following his dad out of the driveway when he heard Ellie yell at him.

"Kyle, you had better remember what I told you about my sister's pony!"

Molly seemed pleased to have someone riding her again. She did hold her head down and kept flipping her ears forward and backwards as she cautiously walked to her new home. Fetch walked right along side of Molly.

When Kyle turned Molly into the driveway, he saw his mom waiting at the front yard gate. He rode Molly to the gate where she took hold of the reins and petted Molly as she gently examined the pony's eyes. Fetch was standing close by watching with interest. After she finished her examination of the new member of the family, she handed Kyle his crutches. Kyle could tell by the look in his mother's eyes that she felt sorry but liked Molly. Jim dismounted and told Mrs. Wyatt.

"I sure hope we are not disappointed. I did have a very nice visit with the Tuckers over a cup of coffee about this polio our children have."

He turned to Kyle and said.

"Let's put Smokey and Molly in the barn. We need to build a rack for your pony's saddle. Remember Mr. Tucker told you to take care of it and keep it oiled."

Kyle's dad started leading Smokey to the barn and was surprised when he looked back and saw Kyle hobbling along with his crutches and Fetch had Molly's reins in his mouth leading Molly. Molly was gently following along. After Molly was in her stall and fed, Kyle and his dad starting building a rack to set the saddle on. Fetch stayed in the stall with Molly and kept a close eye on her. After Molly had eaten her hay and grain, she was turned loose in the barn lot. Fetch stayed right with her. Kyle was surprise when Fetch took hold of Molly's halter and led her over to the water tank for a drink. Kyle's dad was watching also and said.

"I guess Molly has a friend who is going to watch over her and help by being her eyes."

After Kyle was in bed and his parents were swinging on the front porch swing, Fetch was in the barn with Molly. He would come out and do his usual patrolling of the farm, then return to the barn to be with Molly. As Kyle's parents gently swung, they listened to the quietness of the night. Finally Kyle's dad broke the silence and said.

"I told you I had a nice visit with the Tuckers this morning. They wanted to know what we were doing to help Kyle get over the effects of polio. I told them we rub and exercise his legs every night to keep the muscles alive. I also told them I think it is helping him although we are not sure since the progress is so slow. They plan on asking the doctor to remove the cast from Elsie so they can exercise her legs. They are so afraid her legs will just wither and she will never walk again if they stay in the cast."

Mrs. Wyatt said.

"You know Jim I feel everything is going to be alright with Molly and Kyle. I am surprised and happy that Fetch has decided to watch and help Molly. Molly and Fetch act like they are long lost friends."

Jim gave his wife a hug and then they sat and listened to the sounds of the night which included Fetch making his routine patrol from the barn instead of the porch.

Kyle couldn't wait to finish his chores the next morning because he was going to ride Molly around on the farm. After breakfast, he fed Fetch and then headed to the barn to brush Molly. When he finished, his dad saddled Molly and lifted him up into the saddle and handed him the reins. Fetch was right by their side. Kyle's dad cautioned him to ride slow and let Molly get the feel of him as the rider and used to her surroundings. Kyle rode Molly all morning long before he returned to the barn for dinner. After Molly was unsaddled, she was turned out into the pasture to graze and Fetch stayed right by her side. Kyle and his dad watched as Fetch kept Molly away from the barbed wire fence. While the family was eating, Kyle's parents encouraged him to ride Molly to school to get her used to it before school starts.

Fetch stayed by Molly's side and slept in the barn every night with her except when he went to check around the farm to see all was well. Kyle tied a very short rope onto Molly's halter ring so Fetch could lead Molly which he did every day. Kyle did ride Molly to school and back several times before school started with Fetch along side. Kyle's dad had been watching closely and noticed how Molly had complete trust in Kyle and Fetch to guide her when she needed it. He had discussed with Kyle and Mrs. Tucker about letting Kyle ride Molly to school and let Fetch lead Molly home. In the afternoon, they would have Fetch lead Molly back to school to get Kyle when school was done for the day.

Kyle's mom was not in favor of it until her husband said he would follow a short distance behind and watch the first day. On the first day of school Kyle rode Molly out of the driveway and down the road toward school, Fetch was right there beside them. They did not notice Mr. Wyatt following them on Smokey. Before Kyle arrived at school, his dad rode Smokey off into the fence row where he went unnoticed but could watch as Kyle dismounted. After Kyle was steady on his crutches, he handed Fetch the reins and told him.

"Take Molly home Fetch."

Fetch did exactly as he had been told. When they arrived home, Kyle's dad took the saddle off of Molly and gave her a good brushing and Fetch a pat on the head along with words of praise. In the afternoon Molly was saddled and Fetch was handed the reins. Kyle's dad said.

"Go Fetch Kyle."

Fetch did exactly as he had been told. The teacher helped Kyle mount and handed him his crutches. Kyle stopped on the way home and delivered Elsie her home assignments. Ellie again told Kyle.

"You had better take good care of my sister's pony!"

All the neighbors made it a practice to watch for Kyle, Mollie, and Fetch every morning and afternoon. Some of them shook their heads in amazement at how the three seemed to fit together like three peas in a pod. Molly's eyesight was now where she needed Kyle's help directing her with the reins and Fetch helping her find where she needed to go. Fetch seemed to know his friend's eyesight was nearly gone. When the two of them were together and resting, Fetch would tenderly lick Molly's eyes lids as she closed them. Kyle had been trying to keep her eyes from watering and festering. He noticed since Fetch had been keeping Molly's eye lids clean with his licking, her eyes looked clearer. Kyle's mother had noticed it also as she had kept a motherly watch over Molly.

Kyle would pick up Elsie's school homework every morning and deliver her assignments every afternoon. Elsie had her cast removed and had improved enough to sit in a chair by Thanksgiving. It appeared to all that Molly was now totally blind. She was very cautious when she walked. When Christmas vacation arrived, Molly got a rest from the long walk to school but seemed like she missed it. Fetch stayed with her more now and led her with the short halter rope to her water and her feed. Fetch still was the doctor for Molly's eyes by keeping them clean.

Kyle would ride Molly to visit Elsie over Christmas vacation. One day Mr. Tucker asked Kyle if Elsie could go for a ride on Molly. Of course Kyle agreed. Mr. Tucker carried his smiling daughter out of the house and sat her in the saddle for the first time since she had gotten sick. Her legs still were lifeless and she held onto the saddle horn to keep from falling off as her dad took the reins and led Molly around the barnyard under Fetch's watchful eyes. Kyle was glad to see the cold air put the redness in his friend's cheeks and to hear her laughter. She told Kyle.

"This is a great Christmas present."

Ellie still put her hands on her hips and scolded Kyle every chance she got about caring for her sister's pony.

Molly had learned she could depend on Kyle and Fetch to help her find her way. If she moved when they were not there to help she always moved with caution. Molly seemed to enjoy her trips to and from school. As spring approached, Kyle seemed to be gaining strength in his crippled leg. He could now mount Molly without any help from his teacher or dad. Of course part of the reason is his friend Elsie had informed him that Molly could and would kneel onto her front legs which allowed Kyle to crawl in the saddle unassisted. She had told him how to get her to kneel. Kyle continued to visit Elsie every day to pick up and deliver her home work during the remainder of the school year.

Kyle's parents were so proud of Molly. She was such a gentle and trusting pony. They were equally proud of Fetch for his help and care of his friend. Fetch was a continuous helper and companion to Molly. When they rested at night, Molly would nuzzle Fetch as he licked her eyelids. It seemed to give Molly comfort. Kyle's mom would stop by the barn and pet Molly everyday. She had noticed how Molly's eyes were dim and lifeless during the winter months but since spring had arrived she seemed to have a spring in her step and her eyes actually looked as if they were getting better. They were getting clearer looking with a little reflection in them. She knew it would be a miracle if Molly regained some of her vision. She was sure Molly was the reason Kyle was regaining the use of his crippled leg.

On a hot summer Sunday after the morning service at the little country church where every neighbor attended, the ladies were preparing for a church picnic. The men had set up a long table on sawhorses and the ladies spread sheets over the table. As the children played the men sat around and talked. The ladies took fried chicken and potato salad along with all the trimmings from their picnic baskets and set it on the table. Kyle and Elsie had been sitting under a shade tree watching the rest of the children run and play. They both were secretly wishing they could join their friends. Elsie now was wearing leg braces and could use crutches to drag herself around. Kyle noticed their dads had moved off away from the other men and were having a private talk.

The afternoon passed quickly as well as all the fried chicken and potato salad. It was then time for the men to get the ice cream freezers which had been sitting in the shade packed in ice. Kyle ate his home made ice cream so fast it gave him a head ache. When he mentioned it to Elsie, Ellie was standing close by listening and told him.

"That's what you get for being a hog."

She then ran off knowing that her sister and Kyle could not follow and catch her. After the dessert was finished, it was time to put everything away and pack up to go home. It had been a great day for everyone.

That evening after all the evening chores were complete, the family sat on the front porch listening to the sounds of the approaching night. Kyle sat on the edge of the porch and let his legs hang off of the edge. As he sat there, he swung his crippled leg trying to regain the strength in it. He could now put a little weight on it. His parents were slowly swinging and enjoying the cool of the evening. Finally, Kyle's dad broke the evening silence when he said.

"Mr. Tucker told me Elsie would be going to school this fall and Ellie will be starting school. He has been watching how Molly has carried Kyle to and from school and so has the other neighbors. He knows where a pony cart along with a set of pony harnesses is located. The blacksmith has an old cart in an old storage shed and is willing to fix it up and give to us. Another neighbor has the pony harness and has no need for it. He is willing to give it to us also. Mr. Tucker thought maybe Molly could be used along with the cart to carry the children to and from school. He was wondering if we would be willing to see if Molly would let us harness her and hitch her to a cart. He suggested if we agreed to try it, he would talk to the blacksmith about any necessary repairs to the cart and then bring the harness and cart over to try out. You know Kyle, it wouldn't hurt to give it a try before school starts and see if Molly can be used to pull the cart. It will give her time to get used to it. You know Mr. Tucker was nice selling Molly to you for ten cents. If you could give his girls a ride to school everyday, it would give him more time to work in the fields."

Kyle sat quietly for a moment. He could just visualize in his mind Molly pulling the cart. He thought it would be fun and he would enjoy Elsie's company going to school. Kyle then replied.

"I would like to try Dad. Do you think Molly would really pull a cart?"

"I don't think it would hurt to give it a try. It sure would help them out." His dad replied.

Kyle's mom quickly agreed.

One week later, Kyle and his dad had just finished putting a load of alfalfa hay in the barn when Mr. Tucker came rattling in the driveway in his old pickup truck. He had a little pony cart hitched onto the back of the truck and a harness for a pony in the truck bed. After he squeaked to a stop by the barn, he got out and shook Kyle's and Mr. Wyatt's hand.

"If you have time, let's try this harness on Molly and hitch her to the cart." Mr. Tucker said.

Kyle put Molly in her stall and she was soon harnessed. The collar and harness fit perfectly. Molly was led outside and hitched to the pony cart. Molly seemed to be a little nervous with the harness on her when she was first hitched to the cart. Mr. Tucker took hold of her bridle and led her around the barnyard under the watchful eyes of Kyle and Fetch. Molly was at first kind of skittish but soon acted as if she had done this before.

"Let's give Kyle a try driving her with the reins from the cart." Mr. Wyatt said.

After Kyle was safely onboard with the reins in his hand, he spoke to Molly and she pulled the cart like she was enjoying it. Fetch was walking along by her side and watching Molly's every move. Both men agreed Kyle should practice with Molly in the barnyard for a week before he ventured out on the road. This would let Molly get used to pulling the cart and give Kyle experience in driving her.

One week later, Molly pulled the cart to school with Fetch checking on her all the way. As Molly pulled the cart down the road, she was under the watchful eyes of Kyle, Fetch and all the neighbors. One day as Kyle drove Molly down the road, he saw Mr. Tucker standing out by the road waiting for him. When Kyle stopped by Mr. Tucker he saw Elsie and Ellie sitting on the ditch bank.

"Are you ready for a couple of passengers?" He asked.

Kyle readily agreed and the girls were soon tucked safely in the cart along side of Kyle. Mr. Tucker followed along behind on a horse to make sure all was well. He soon found out he was not needed. Kyle and Fetch had everything under control except for Ellie's scolding of Kyle about his driving of Molly.

When school started again, the sight of these children in a cart being pulled by a pony and a watchful dog trotting close by became a daily sight. Fetch would still lead Molly home after the children arrived at school. In the afternoon, he would be seen faithfully leading Molly back to school to bring the children home. This was the beginning of daily ritual during the school year.

The men in the community got together and decided a shed should be attached to the woodshed at school for Molly and Fetch to stay in when the roads were muddy and the weather was bad. This would allow Molly and Fetch to make only one round trip a day during bad weather. They all donated material for the shed and hay and straw for Molly. The teacher agreed to have the older school boys help unhitch Molly in the morning and hitch her back to the cart in the afternoon. This proved to work out great. All the children enjoyed helping care for them and that they were fed and watered. Molly and Fetch soon became a part of the school. The students liked caring for them so much they would wish for bad weather so Molly and Fetch could stay at school during the day.

Weeks led to months and months led to years. During this period of time, Kyle had regained enough strength in his leg to walk without crutches. Elsie could stand on her legs but still required crutches to help her along her way. They both agreed how lucky they were. Their childhood friend, Bobby, was free from the iron lung and was now in heaven.

Molly remained a faithful and gentle pony but was showing a little gray on her muzzle. She had regained a little of her eyesight. She still had to depend on Kyle and Fetch going to and from school. She could find her way from the barn to her water and could see just enough to keep from running into large objects. Fetch still had to keep her away from the barbed wire fences.

When Ellie was in the sixth grade, she suddenly decided to quit nagging Kyle about taking care of her sister's pony. Now she could be heard telling him everyday.

"When I grow up I am going to marry you Kyle."

Kyle would just grin at her and Elsie would roll her eyes at her younger sister as they rode together down the country road. Molly strolled along with Fetch at her side; both seemed to be enjoying their stroll together.

"Next year Elsie, we will be going to high school in town. I guess Molly and Fetch can then rest and enjoy their time together. It is too far for them to take us and they have earned a vacation." Kyle said.

Kyle then looked at Ellie and said.

"Am I taking good enough care of your sister's pony to satisfy you?"

Before Kyle knew what was happening. Ellie reached over and gave him a kiss on the cheek and said."

I'm still going to marry you someday.

ANGIE'S PLAYMATE

ANGIE'S mother was curiously looking out the kitchen window as she was preparing lunch. She was watching little Angie playing in the backyard. Angie was talking to someone but she saw no one else in the back yard. She watched as Angie would run and jump as if she was playing with a friend. Oh well, it is probably just another imaginary friend her daughter has found. Angie was now doing cart-wheels with her friend. She was laughing and having so much fun.

Angie and her friend were busy all morning playing together. They did tricks together on the monkey bars and then would swing for a while. They were such good friends and tried to take turns sliding down the slide. They did take time out to have a little tea party in the back yard when Angie's mother brought out some cookies and milk for refreshments. They set close together and shared the cookies and milk. One would not eat without the other. They both laughed together as they sat and enjoyed their pretend tea party with milk and cookies. Angie ate what was left over because her friend was too full to eat anymore.

They were very close friends and what one did, so did the other. They played in the sun and never sat under the shade tree. It seemed as if Angie's little friend did not like shade. When they rested together they would set on the porch steps in the sunshine talking and laughing. Angie loved to make different motions with her hands and watch as her friend did the same. Sometimes she would try to fool her friend and ballet or run real fast trying to do it without her friend doing the same thing. No matter how hard she tried she never could do anything without her friend doing the same.

When Angie's mother called her to come in to eat lunch, Angie asked her friend to join her but her friend refused. She followed her to the backdoor and no further. Angie told her little friend she had to go in but asked if she would come back and play after she had eaten her lunch and taken a nap. When Angie stepped into the house her little friend was disappointed her playmate could not stay outside. She disappeared but would be back and ready to play when Angie came out. After Angie had eaten her lunch, she laid down to take a short nap. She had a soccer game that afternoon and her mother wanted her to rest before the game.

After Angie had finished her nap she put on her soccer uniform and shoes. She looked for her friend on the back porch but she was no where to be found. Angie was sad because she wanted her friend to go to the soccer game with her. She was on the team just like Angie. When it was time to go to practice, Angie stepped out on the front porch and into the sunshine. A huge smile crossed her face when she saw her friend waiting for her on the front porch. Angie jumped off the front porch steps and was closely followed by her companion. They ran step for step toward the car. Angie was in the lead and opened the door for her friend.

When they arrived at the soccer field, both jumped out of the car and ran over to where the rest of the team was waiting. When the game started, Angie made sure her friend was on the field with her. When she jumped so did her little friend. When she kicked and chased the soccer ball, her friend was right by her side. When Angie was replaced on the field by a team mate her friend went to the bench with her for a much needed rest. Sometimes the coach would have to go and fetch Angie back from the other end of the field to get her in position. It seemed that sometimes Angie's interest was on her friend and not on the game. When she would flip her pony tail, so would her friend.

One time Angie stood in the center of the field with her friend while the rest of the players were on the other end of the field. Angie and her friend also were doing a dance routine to the enjoyment of the crowd during the game. She would stand on one leg and kick the other leg out in front of her. She watched as her friend did the same. She then danced like a cheerleader and moved her arms as if she had pompoms. Her friend followed her in the dance routine as if they were one. She raised her hands over head and clapped them with her friend. Then it was time to do jumping jacks as she faced her friend.

All of a sudden a passing cloud removed Angie's friend from in front of her and from the game. Angie started to cry and nothing would cheer her up. She was replaced on the field and as she sat on the bench, the sunshine reappeared and so did her friend. Angie's tears were replaced with a huge smile. Unknown to the other team they had been playing against a team that had an extra player on the field. When the game was over, Angie and her little friend lined up with the rest of the team and traded goodwill with the other team with high fives. Then it was time to celebrate the win with ice cream. Angie ate her friend's ice cream since she felt her friend did not like ice cream, plus she had left the soccer field without the coaches' permission. Friends are supposed to help one another and they did for the rest of Angie's lifetime.

A STORY TELLING PUPPET

A little hand puppet named Happy crawled into Gramps canvas bag and was carried to a kindergarten classroom. When he arrived in the classroom he crawled out of the bag and was soon perched proudly on Gramps hand looking at the kindergarten students. He introduced himself in a grouchy voice as, "Happy." The students told him.

"You don't sound very happy; you are grouchy."

He replied.

"I am happy and you should not smile or it will crack your face."

The children did not believe him and let him know all about it. They told him.

"You are all wrong, our face will not crack."

He replied.

"Sit down in your seats. I have a story to tell you. Gramps has been doing all the reading of stories and telling some of his own. Now it is my turn."

All the class let Happy know he could not tell a story.

He replied in his grouchy voice.

"I can and will tell my story and it is true. Once upon a time there was an old mangy wolf trotting in the woods looking for something to eat when he saw a little girl dressed in red carrying a basket. He jumped out of the woods in front of her onto the path she was following. He said.

"Hey, what do you have in your basket?"

She replied.

"My mom told me not to talk to strangers, but you can look in the basket and see for yourself. You will see it is some stuff for my grandma."

The mangy old wolf lifted the cover off the basket and looked inside. He sniffed it with his long hairy nose and put the cover back on the basket. He said.

"I am hungry for a ham sandwich. Do you know where some little pigs live?"

The little girl in red knew where the pigs lived but they were her friends. She pointed down a path which led to the bear's house as she said.

"If you follow that path over there for a mile, you will find their house on the right. You can't miss it."

The old mangy wolf licked his lips and thanked her as he reached into her basket and took out a couple cookies to eat for dessert after he had his ham sandwich. He trotted on down the path the little girl in red had pointed to. As he trotted along, he tried to whistle to pass the time but he could not pucker his lips. He drooled as he thought about the ham sandwich he would be eating soon. About a mile down the path he saw a nice house on the right. As he trotted up to the front door he could smell the aroma of food in the air. He was drooling heavily as he knocked on the front door and said.

"Delivery boy, I have a package for you but you must sign for it."

Inside the house were some bears looking at their steaming breakfast bowls. They had just finished cooking some hot cereal on the stove and it was too hot to eat. One of the bears looked through the peek hole in the front door and saw a mangy old wolf standing outside drooling on their front porch. The bears yelled. "Go away!"

The mangy old wolf yelled as loud as he could.

"I know you are a pig trying to sound like a bear. If you don't let me in I will huff and puff and blow your house down."

The old grandpa bear told the other bears.

"Stand back; if that mangy old wolf wants to huff and puff, I will let him huff and puff on our hot cereal to cool it."

Old Grandpa Bear jerked open the door and before the startled mangy old wolf could move, Grandpa grabbed him by the scruff of his mangy neck and carried him in the house and into the kitchen. He told the wolf.

"Okay, you wanted to huff and puff, well just huff and puff on our hot cereal until it is cool enough for us to eat."

The old mangy wolf huffed and puffed like he had never huffed and puffed before in his life. When he had the cereal cool enough for the bears to eat, Grandpa stretched the old mangy wolf out like a rubber band while holding him by the scruff of his neck and the tip of his tail. He had one of the bears open the kitchen window. He then shot the old mangy wolf out the window like an arrow. The wolf sailed through the air and hit a tree nose first fifty feet away. As the bears ate their cereal, the old mangy wolf limped off into the woods hungry and beat up.

He had lost the cookies he had taken from the little girl dressed in red. He decided to look for her and eat the rest of the stuff in the basket to ease his hunger. He still wanted a ham sandwich though. As he limped through the woods he saw a little boy leading a cow. He decided a steak sandwich would taste just as good. Just as he stepped out of the woods and onto the path the boy with the cow was on, he saw a strange little man buying the cow for beans. He knew he could steal the cow from that strange looking fellow.

When the old mangy wolf threatened the strange little man to give him the cow or he would bite him, the strange little man grabbed the mangy wolf by his tail and tied it in a knot. The wolf's tail was still hurting from the bear twanging him through the air like an arrow by stretching him like a rubber band while holding him by the scruff of his neck and his tail. The strange little man then stretched the wolf's ears under his jaws and tied them together. The strange little man hummed to the mangy wolf all the time he was tying his ears together and tying a knot in his tail. He then stepped back and smiled as looked at the wolf. His tied down ears reminded him of the long ear flaps on a winter hat. The mangy old wolf never heard a sound as the strange man left leading the cow down the path and disappeared around a bend.

The mangy wolf decided to look for the boy with the beans. Maybe he could steal the beans and at least make himself some bean soup. As he was limping through the woods, he could not wag his tail since it hurt and had a knot in it. He could not hear a thing since his ears were tied together under his jaws. When he tried to open his mouth to pant it stretched his ears. He was a mournful looking creature. He finally came to a house where some little men lived with a girl with blonde hair. He did not stop there because he remembered what strange little men do to wolf's tails and ears.

Just when he was about to give up and call it a bad day, he saw some goats on a hill looking across a stream at a greener pasture. Oh well, he could settle for some goat cheese or goat stew. Just as he was limping toward them, they crossed a bridge one at a time to the greener pasture. The old mangy wolf followed them and when he was on the bridge, an ugly looking creature came out from under the bridge and grabbed the mangy old wolf by his tail and swung him around and around as fast as he could. The knot in the tail kept the wolf from slipping out of the ugly looking creatures hands. Then he let go of the old mangy wolf's sore tail with a knot in it and sent him sailing through the air toward the deep cold water in the stream. When the wolf tried to open his mouth to howl, he could not hear himself since it stretched his ears tighter over his ear holes so he could not hear himself. Since he could not hear himself scream, he could not hear himself splash down in the cold deep water. He never got any water in his ears holes since they were tightly covered."

Happy looked at the fidgeting kindergarten class. They all raised their hands and each one told him.

"You messed up different stories and that is not how they go!"

He knew they did not believe him but he didn't care. It was about all the stories he had heard told to the class as he hid in the canvas bag. He told them in his grouchy voice.

"I can not help it if all of you have not listened and can't remember the stories as well as I do! I am not finished with my story anyway. Let me see where I was at before all your fidgeting around interrupted me. Oh yes, the mangy old wolf swam to the shore and tried to shake the water off of himself. The knot on his tail swung back and forth and beat him so much he tried to howl but he could not hear himself. He walked and walked and finally came to a house way out in the country. A man lived there with his daughters. He had swiped a rose from an ugly guy and now he had to have one of his daughters go live with the ugly guy. When the man saw the mangy old wolf an idea popped into his mind. He grabbed the wolf and put a girl's wig on him. It fit great since the wolf's ears were tied together. He dressed the wolf in a pretty gown and high heel shoes. Since the wolf didn't have lips that would pucker to whistle, the man smeared lipstick around the wolf's mouth. He carried the wolf over to the ugly guys place on a horse and knocked on the door. When the ugly guy answered the door, the man shoved the wolf into the guy's house as he told him this was his daughter. Then the man jumped on his horse and spurred it to get away quickly.

The ugly guy was glad to see the young lady in his house. He took the wolf into his arms and tried to kiss him. The wolf didn't have any lips to pucker up to kiss. As he squirmed to get away from the ugly guy, his wig fell off. The ugly guy saw he had been tricked so he grabbed the wolf by his tail and tied down ears and shot him like an arrow into his rose garden. The wolf wanted to howl from all the thorns sticking in him but he could not hear himself howl with pain. One rose became entangled in the knot in his tail. He could not undo the knot in his tail or his ears since he has no fingers.

He trotted down the road until he saw the girl dressed in red going into a house. He crawled up to a window and peeked in. There sat an old lady and the girl in red eating goodies from the basket. He went around to the front porch and knocked on the door as he yelled.

"Let me in to share your goodies or I will huff and puff and blow your house in."

The little girl dressed in red said to the old lady.

"Grandma, that sounds like the wolf who stole a couple of your cookies."

Granny grabbed her kitchen broom and jerked the door open before the mangy old wolf could move.

She jumped out on the porch with her broom and gave the wolf a whipping he will never forget. The wolf jumped down off the porch and ran as fast as he could into the woods with the rose stem still sticking in the knot of his tail and his ears still tied together. Granny had beaten all the rose petals off the rose stem with her broom. The mangy old wolf did discover he could run faster with his ears tied down and they made him look like he was wearing a race car driver's helmet. It just had not been a good day for him. Children, now that is the end of the story."

Happy bowed and crawled back into Gramps canvas bag.

The students were all shaking their heads and wanted to tell Happy what they thought of his story, but they knew their teacher would not let them.

GIT

He was snuggled between his brothers and sisters when he felt hands closed around his full mid-section. He felt himself being lifted in the air and the next thing he knew he was looking into the eyes of a child. He heard a little voice say.

"I want this one daddy."

He started squirming in the small hands and tried to lick the face he was looking into. He was then held in two arms and tightly held to the child's chest as he was carried out of the yard. He was soon in a car and going for a ride but he knew not where.

He whimpered as he rode in the young boys arms. He already missed his mother and brothers and sisters. He was carried into another backyard and placed in a dog house. He heard the father tell the boy.

"This pup will have to stay outside. You know your mother does not like animals in the house. What are you going to name him?"

The little boy thought a moment and then answered.

"I don't know. I think I will wait a while and see what he reminds me of."

The puppy cried all night and kept the neighbors awake. They were not very happy. The next morning the puppy dug in the flower bed and howled for his mother. The boy's mother took her broom and swatted as she scolded the puppy for getting in her flower bed. As she swatted him with the broom she yelled.

"Git."

For the next week the puppy constantly stayed in trouble because of his inquisitiveness. He was swatted with the broom and told to, "Git," so much he thought his name was Git. The boy did not take care of the puppy as he had promised his dad when they brought him home. After a week, the mother demanded the puppy must leave. She was tired of it digging in her flower bed and the neighbors complaining about his howling. Her demands made the little boy sad. The little boy carried the puppy to the car where his dad was waiting. They drove out into the country and dropped the puppy off in a ditch in front of a farm house. The scared little pup crawled out of the ditch in time to see the car going down the road. He ran trying to catch it but was soon lost in the dust.

He spent the night shivering as he lay in the weeds in the ditch hungry and lonely. The next morning he followed his nose to a farm house where breakfast was being cooked. He scratched on the back screen door and was met with a boot kicking him in the side and telling him.

"Git."

He ran out to the barn and was helping himself to some milk the farmer had put in a pan for the cats. He hardly got to taste it before a snarling momma cat attacked him and ran him out of the barn with his tail between his legs. He ran to get away and was soon lost in tall grass. He lay down and rested for a while. He was so hungry and thirsty. Finally, he started walking and crying. He had not idea where he was at, but he knew he had to find some food and water. He soon came to a little creek and quenched his thirst. He followed the creek but found nothing to eat. When darkness came he curled up in dry leaves under a fallen log. He woke up itching. The chiggers and ticks had found the poor half starved puppy and were having themselves a picnic.

A week later he found another farm house and this time was swatted with a broom by the lady of the house and told to.

"Git."

He did find some food scraps that had been thrown out for the chickens to eat. He hungrily started eating among the fluttering chickens. He was soon attacked by the rooster and forced to flee. As he was running away from the flock of chickens, he heard a loud noise and his left hind leg hurt. When he got to the end of the driveway, he crawled in the weed filled ditch. He started to lick his leg and found strange tasting moisture on it. He finally dragged himself out of the weeds and onto the edge of the road. He was so weak from starvation he never noticed the car which stopped near by. He felt hands pick him up ever so gently. He heard a gentle voice say.

"Who would mistreat a puppy like this? You are half starved, eaten up with ticks and chiggers, and it also appears someone has shot you."

He looked through matted eyes and saw the face of an older lady. She was not scolding him or beating him with a broom like the other ladies had. He had never been treated this way before. He weakly stuck out his tongue and licked the hands which were holding him. She placed him on the floorboard of her car on an old sweater. She talked gently to him as she drove down the road. His little tail wagged without him even being aware it was moving. When the lady arrived at her house she took the puppy to an enclosed back porch. She fed the little fellow first, then she bathed him and put medicine on him to get rid of the chiggers and ticks. She examined the bullet wound and found the bullet had passed through his leg. She bandages it and placed the puppy in a basket next to her old rocking chair on the old sweater she had carried in her car.

She looked at her little companion and said.

"You are just what I need. It has been so lonely around here and now I have someone to take care of and love. I know you have been told to git so much you must think that is your name. I guess I will just name you Git."

Git looked up into her kind eyes and wagged his little tail. He now had another momma to love and share his life with.

JOEY

LITTLE Joey was sitting on a stump in the backyard drawing pictures in the dirt with a stick. The morning air had a chill in it and he was shivering in his thin shirt. He did not want to wake his mother since she was not feeling well. Joey heard a cough and looked in the direction it came from. He saw Miss Betty feeding her cat next door. Joey ran over to the fence to talk with her as he did every day. He yelled.

"Hi Miss Betty; are you feeding your cat? That cat sure is lucky to get to eat. I didn't get any breakfast this morning. My mom is not feeling well so I went outside without breakfast so she could get rest."

Miss Betty smiled to herself since Joey's story was the same everyday. Everyday when she goes out to feed the cat, Joey is waiting because he knows she will invite him over for a snack. Of course she enjoys his company and she feels sorry for the young man. Since she retired from teaching school she found she missed the children. Joey helped fill an empty void in her life. She also knew Joey's dad had not been in his life since he was one year old. He had just packed and left looking for work one day and Joey's mother had not heard from him since. She became depressed and had taken a wrong path in life. Miss Betty was glad she could help watch Joey and to have him for company.

Miss Betty invited Joey into her house and gave him a cup of hot chocolate and a bowl of oatmeal. She felt he needed some good nourishment. Joey was a very active boy and found more ways to entertain himself. She loved to set in her rocking chair on the back porch and watch him play. When he would see her working in her yard, Joey would offer to help her. She always rewarded him with a snack and something to drink. One day as Joey sat on her back porch steps petting the cat and visiting with her he asked.

"Can I call you Grandma Betty, Miss Betty?"

She was taken by surprise. She paused for a moment and then a gentle smile crossed her faced as she replied.

"Nothing would please me more Joey. I don't know of any other boy I would rather be Grandma Betty to."

Joey shyly got up from the step and walked over to her and gave her a hug. The hug melted her heart and she knew she loved this young man and would help him anyway she could. Yes, she was very fortunate to be living next door where she could be a grandma and maybe help him down the road of life. She looked at him and said.

"You know Joey, I have a cake which is just waiting to be eaten."

He took hold of her hand and helped her out of her rocking chair. They walked hand in hand into the house to see about the cake.

The next day while Joey was playing pretend in his backyard, Miss Betty slipped out her front door with half of a cake and went to visit with Joey's mom. When Joey's mom answered her door, her hair was a mess and she was dressed in a rumpled gown. Miss Betty met her with a smile. They sat at a cluttered kitchen table and drank black coffee and ate cake like good neighbors. Miss Betty asked Joey's mom if she could take Joey to town and buy him a new shirt and jeans. She told her.

"I am retired and Joey is so much company to me. He has been helping me do my yard work and I want to get him something for helping me."

Joey's mom thought a while and then replied.

"We don't want any charity from you but if Joey has been working for you then it is okay with me if you buy him some clothes. Heaven knows he needs them."

Joey interrupted their conversation when he came in the back door with rumpled hair and a dirty face. He had come in to get a drink of water to quench his thirst. Joey's mom scolded him for slamming the screen door when he came in. Joey looked at Miss Betty and said.

"Hi Grandma Betty, that cake sure looks good."

Joey's mom told Joey.

"Go wash you hands and face and then maybe you can have some. Why did you call Miss Betty, Grandma?"

Miss Betty said.

"He asked me one day if he could call me that while we were visiting. I told him that nothing would please me more. You know he is a lot of help to me and is just like family. Without him to help me and visit with I would lead a very lonely life."

Joey's mom poured herself another cup of black coffee and shrugged her shoulders as she mumbled.

"He doesn't have a grandma so I guess it is okay with me if it is with you."

Joey came out of the bathroom with part of the dirt missing from his face and wiping his hands on his pant leg. He looked at the cake as he pulled out a chair to sit at the table. He had tasted plenty of Grandma's Betty's cakes and he knew this one would taste just as good. His mother poured him a glass of water as Grandma Betty cut him a piece of cake. Joey thanked her and then made the cake quickly disappear. Then he was off to the backyard again and his game of pretend. Miss Betty and Joey's mother continued to visit over coffee. As Miss Betty was getting ready to leave, she invited Joey's mother to come over and visit anytime. Miss Betty went home and sat on her back porch in her rocking chair and watched Joey play his games of pretend.

The next afternoon Miss Betty took Joey shopping for new clothes. She bought him two shirts and two pair of jeans along with socks and a new pair of shoes. They stopped at the ice cream store and each ate a dish of ice cream. Joey took his time eating the ice cream. He very seldom had ice cream to eat and wanted it to last as long as he could. After they had finished their ice cream, they walked to the grocery store. Joey pushed the shopping cart for her as she shopped. After they had went through the check out, Joey carried some of the groceries for her to the car. When they arrived back home he carried the groceries into the house for her. Then he took his new clothes and ran home as fast as his little legs would carry him. He was very proud of them and wanted to show them to his mom.

After Joey had shown his clothes to his mother, he put them away in his bedroom. He went outside and was playing in the backyard games of pretend. He saw Grandma Betty watching him as he played. He stopped long enough to thank her again for the new clothes and to wave at her. She waved back and gave him a smile. When the sun was disappearing and darkness was starting to settle over his backyard, his mom told him it was time to come in and take his bath. After he had eaten a meager supper, he took his bath and his mom tucked him into bed. A short time later he heard the front door close as he did every night. He knew his mother was going to where ever she went ever night. He was glad Grandma Betty lived next door.

The next morning after he was dressed and had brushed his teeth, he went into the backyard. He hoped Grandma Betty was outside so he could talk to her and maybe have breakfast with her. He walked over to the fence. He did not see her in her flower garden or setting on the back porch. He listened carefully when he thought he heard a moan. He looked closely to see where the sound was coming from. He then saw her lying at the bottom of the porch steps. He ran over to where she was lying with her cat next to her. Joey tried to help her but she could not get up. She had been lying there all night. Joey ran into her house and called 911.

After the ambulance left, Joey ran home and woke his mom. He told her about Miss Betty and asked her.

"Can we go to the hospital to make sure she is alright?"

Joey's mom did not have a telephone so later in the morning she walked next door to Miss Betty's house and called the hospital. She was told that Miss Betty had a broken arm, sprained ankle and a possible concussion. They were going to keep her in the hospital overnight for observation. After Joey and his mom had eaten lunch, they went to the hospital to visit Miss Betty. Miss Betty was happy to see them, especially Joey. She asked Joey's mom if she would give her a ride home when she was released. She thanked Joey for calling 911.

After Miss Betty was home, she needed assistance. Joey had asked his mom to help Grandma Betty which she reluctantly agreed. Joey helped everyday and made her day pass faster by just visiting with her. He fed and watered the cat, watered the flowers and ran all the errands for Grandma Betty. Grandma Betty hired Joey's mom to help her until she could take care of herself. Joey's mom became very fond of Miss Betty. She really had never taken the time to know her neighbor like her son had. Miss Betty and Joey's mom had many conversations about Joey. Joey's mom soon realized she had not been involved in her son's life as she should have been.

After Miss Betty had her cast removed and her sprained ankle had healed, she called a friend and arranged a job interview for Joey's mom.

Miss Betty and Joey's mom went shopping together where Miss Betty bought Joey's mom a pretty dress for the interview. Of course they had to stop and have a dish of ice cream with Joey. Joey had noticed since Miss Betty had been hurt, he never heard the front door close at night after he was in bed and he always found breakfast on the table when he got up in the morning.

After Joey's mom was dressed to go to her interview, she paused and looked at herself in the mirror. Joey was watching her and said.

"Mom, you sure are pretty!"

He had never told her that before. She looked closer at herself in the mirror and saw a lady in a pretty dress. This lady was not wearing the bright red lipstick and red rouge as she had seen her wear in the mirror before. She smiled at herself and turned to give her son a hug. She said.

"Joey, while I am gone for the interview your Grandma Betty wants you to stay with her. She needs some help eating ice cream and cake."

Joey gave his mom a kiss and out the back door he ran to go help his Grandma.

JUST A STICK

BILLY was playing in his favorite Oak tree in his grandpa's backyard. Billy's grandpa was sitting in the shade of the tree as his grandson played. Billy saw a dead branch a little higher up in the tree. He climbed up to it and kicked it as hard as he could. The dead branch broke off and fell to the ground just barely missing his grandpa and making Queen open one eye. Billy watched as Grandpa got up and walked over to the dead branch and picked it up. He saw Queen, Grandpa's old hunting dog, yawn and stretch as she watched him go get the branch. She never moved from where she had been lying by him. He examined it a moment and then carried it back over to where he had been sitting. He took out his pocket knife and started whittling on it. Billy watched from his place high up in the tree.

Finally, curiosity got the best of Billy. He just had to see what his grandpa saw in the dead branch. When he reached the ground safely, he walked over to where his grandpa was sitting and whittling. He paused for a second and looked at his grandson. He smiled at him and said.

"Thanks for the treasure stick you found hiding up there in the tree."

Billy looked at his grandpa and then the stick he held in his hand. He said.

"Grandpa, it is just a stick."

Grandpa replied.

"Billy, every stick is a treasure stick. They all have their own little treasure hid within them. Sit down here and I will show you."

Billy sat down by the tree trunk and watched as his grandpa carved and old Indian's face close to the larger end of the stick. He wanted Queen to come over and sit by him. Queen was content to lay by Grandpa, plus she knew Billy would want her to fetch sticks. She kept the fetch stick Grandpa had made years ago hid between her paws so Billy would not see it. When his grandpa was done with the face, he stood up and pointed the stick to the east, then south, then west, and then north. Billy watched as his grandpa closed his eyes and chanted like an Indian. He listened as his grandpa talked about all the buffalo which had disappeared from the Great Plains and how he used to hunt them riding his Indian pony. He watched as his grandpa pointed to the north and talked of the great hunting grounds where all the buffalo have gone. Billy did not see his grandpa peek out of one eye at him as he was pointing to the great hunting grounds. Grandpa saw that Billy was listening intently. Grandpa then lowered the stick and started to chant again as he did an Indian dance around an imaginary campfire.

Finally, Grandpa sat back down in the shade and started whittling some more. Billy watched as his grandpa whittled on the opposite side of the stick from the old Indian face. Billy just had to ask Grandpa.

"What are you whittling now?"

Grandpa kept right on whittling as he answered.

"A whistle stick; everyone needs a whistle stick. If you have a dog you can whistle for him to come to you. If you are lost in the woods you can blow the whistle stick to let people know where you are at. I was lost in a blinding snow storm and it was forty below zero. I had no idea which direction my home was. Old Queen here was home taking care of her puppies. I blew the whistle on my whistle stick as hard as I could. Well Billy, you know high pitch sounds hurt dog's ears. Old Queen heard the whistle and it hurt her ears. She started howling and I followed her howls and found my way home. Queen and the whistle stick had saved my life."

Grandpa started whittling on the other end of the stick and soon had it shaped like he wanted it. He paused for a moment to scratch Queen behind her ears. Then he trimmed the places where little twig branches had started to grow. He would whittle and then hold the stick out and look at it. Then he would continue with his whittling. As he whittled he said to Billy.

"I once made an Indian flute from a dead Arkansas Red Cedar branch. When I was finished with it, I gently blew into it and the mournful sound it made carried on the wind to the Indians in the Happy Hunting ground. When I lay down at night and looked at the stars in the heavens, I could hear the sounds of their cedar flutes carrying on the wind to me as they play. Cedar branches have their own treasure waiting to be found in each one.

I once took a stick and whittled a walking staff with it. With that staff I would herd sheep. I used it to keep wolves away from the flock also. Once while walking in the woods, a bear leaped out at me. I took my staff and fought him off. He chewed the end of my staff badly but when I got back to my camp, I took my knife and whittled it until it was smooth. I still have that staff in my work shop. Some of the teeth marks are still in the staff. Yes sir, every stick is different and has a special use hiding in it. That makes each stick special and a treasure. This stick now is a walking stick, a whistle stick, and a stick to talk to the Indian tribes of the past. The picture of the old Indian chief makes it an Indian stick and a medicine stick.

Billy, this stick is now your treasure stick. You can even make it into a pony and ride it. When I was your age, I had me the fastest stick horse alive. We herded cattle together and chased outlaws. I still have him but he is retired and stays out in the pasture for a deserved rest. I even used a treasure stick for a sword. I had many sword fights when I was in the foreign legion. I rode my stick horse into battle with my stick sword raised in the air as we charged the enemy.

I even used the stick as a bat to play stick ball with. There is no such thing as, "Just a stick." They all are very special. You know the one I have now that I use for a cane? I call it my nature stick because I can go for a walk with old Queen and listen to the birds and watch all the animals scurry around. It helps me enjoy Mother Nature as Queen and I just saunter along looking and listening. I think the name Nature Stick is a fitting name for my walking stick. I use it to turn over leaves and see what is hiding under them. You would be amazed at what hides under leaves.

Grandpa stood up and as he handed Billy the stick with all its hidden treasures he said.

"Let's go and see what treats your Grandma has for us to eat. I sure am powerful hungry after traveling to far away place while I was whittling and talking to you." Queen got up and stretched as she yawned. She had heard Grandpa tell all these stories before to his other grandchildren. She followed them up onto the back porch and laid down to wait for them. She knew she was not allowed in the house. She also knew she would get a treat when Billy and Grandpa came back outside. She lay in the sun and tucked her fetch stick between her front paws and then laid her head down on her paws to help hide it. She closed her eyes; she knew it wasn't, "just a stick."

THE BEST CHRISTMAS EVER

GRANDPA Brady sat in his rocking chair watching as his granddaughter lay on an old army cot eating hot chicken noodle soup. He was contemplating how to tell her there would be no Christmas this year. She had broken her thigh bone while playing on the school ground. Two weeks after her leg had been put in a cast she came down with chicken pox. She was more concerned that she would not be able to take part in the Christmas play with her Kindergarten classmate than in her illness. Grandpa Brady has no insurance, and she is his responsibility and has been since she was two years old. He watched as little Becky finished her soup. He took a wash cloth and washed her hands and face. When he had taken a towel and dried her hands and face, he bent over and kissed her on the forehead. He took the empty soup dish and spoon then washed it along with his supper dish and spoon.

Unknown to Grandpa Brady, Becky's teacher along with the teacher and class in the next room were planning a surprise for their classmate. They each brought a present to school for Becky and practiced singing Christmas carols every school day. The parents were so proud their children wanted to share Christmas with their less fortunate friend. A Christmas tree was donated along with a box of battery operated candles. Food was collected for Becky's grandpa to be delivered along with the presents when the class went to carol Becky.

When he was through in the kitchen, he turned out the kitchen light and returned to Becky's side. He sat in his rocking chair for a while trying to think what to tell his precious granddaughter. He cleared his throat as he took out his big red handkerchief and dried the tears from his eyes. Finally, after fighting with himself inside he said.

"Becky, I have something to tell you which hurts me very, very much. There will not be a Christmas in this house this year. What money we have needs to be saved for our necessities. I am so sorry."

He blew his nose and put his handkerchief back in his pocket. Becky reached over and patted her grandpa's hand. She said.

"That is okay Grandpa."

Grandpa Brady got up from his rocking chair and pulled the covers up and tucked Becky in. She lay on her cot and listened as Grandpa finished his evening chores. She closed her eyes tight to keep the tears from flowing. She pulled the curtain back next to her cot and made a wish on the first star she saw.

"I wish my Grandpa would have the best Christmas ever this year."

She watched the star for a moment then closed the curtain to help keep the cold out. She thought she heard bells ringing and children singing. They were singing the same Christmas carols she had practiced singing with her classmates for the Christmas program. She thought she was just hearing things. She pulled back the curtain just a little and was surprised to see her classmates along with the kindergarten class in the room next to hers singing with their teachers as they walked into her front yard. She pulled the curtain all the way open as she yelled.

"Grandpa, come in here."

Grandpa thought he had heard children singing but thought it was his imagination playing tricks on him. He hurried into the front room where Becky was looking out of the front window. He was surprised to see all the children in the front yard carrying presents and a small Christmas tree. Becky and Grandpa Brady watched as they set the Christmas tree on the front porch and then put the presents under it. The teachers then handed each student a little battery operated candle. The children held their little candles high and sang as they stood in front of Becky's window.

Grandpa reached over and opened the window so Becky could hear her friends sing. He put a shawl over Becky's head and shoulders to keep her warm. When the carolers started singing Becky joined in. They were singing the carols she had practiced with them for the Christmas program. They sang, "Let It Snow," "Jingle Bells," "Joy to the World," "Do You See What I See," "Rudolph," "Silent Night," "Joy to the World," "Oh Christmas Tree," "Go tell it on the mountain," "Deck the halls," and "We wish you a Merry Christmas."

When the carolers finished, they each picked up a Christmas present from under the Christmas tree on the front porch. After they had picked up a present, each one then walked by the open front room window and handed Becky their present as they wished her a Merry Christmas. Becky thanked each caroling student and the teachers. She turned to her grandpa and said.

"Grandpa, this is the best Christmas ever!"

THE CANDY TREE

LITTLE Eldo had just gotten out of kindergarten class for elves. He did not like school at all. His classmates made fun of him because sometimes he was just slow to learn and sometimes he just could not remember. Part of the reason could be Eldo was a daydreamer. It was so hard to keep his mind in the classroom when there was so much going on outside in the great big beautiful outdoors. Eldo had his own secret little hiding place in the northern woods where he lived. Everyday after school, he would walk to his secret hiding place where the school bullies and his classmates could not find him. There he would eat the dessert he had saved from his lunch. He was sniffling as usual from being bullied at school as he trudged through the woods.

When he got to his secret hiding place, he crawled in where no one could see him. He opened his lunch sack and took out his left-over dessert. Eldo loved sweets and he had a sweet tooth the size of the moon his momma would say. As he was eating, he let his mind drift off to never-never land where he wanted to live. He felt something land on his head and then he heard it bounce into the leaves. He looked down and saw a seed like he had never seen before. It was shiny and smelled very sweet. It smelled so good he picked it up and started to put it in his mouth to taste.

He stopped before he could get it in his mouth. He heard someone walking in the leaves toward his hiding place. He peeked out from his hiding place and saw no one. He thought it was the school bullies and they must have followed him after school. He hid the seed under the leaves and crawled out of the other side of his hiding place and crawled in a hollow tree. Beth, the little Christmas Angel from Toyland had dropped the special seed from her perch high above. She watched as Eldo examined it and started to taste it. She was horrified when she seen him start to put it in his mouth to taste. She had not dropped it on him for him to eat. It was a special seed and just for him to plant. She was the one making the leaves sound as if they were being walked in toward his hiding place. After she saw the seed had been safely hidden and she knew she had fooled Eldo, she flew off toward her home at the North Pole.

Eldo sat in the hollow log and listened. He did not want his secret hiding place found. He sat silently and when he was sure no one was close by, he peeked out. He saw no one and decided to run home instead of returning to his favorite place. He sure did not want to take a chance on anyone finding his special seed. He arrived home breathless and went straight to his bedroom. He changed from his school clothes and put on his everyday clothes. After he had changed he went into the kitchen where his mother was preparing supper and sat down at the table. She gave him a fresh baked cookie and a pat on his head.

She could tell the bullies had picked on him again today at school. She could also tell something special had happened in his life. He had a sparkle in his eyes. When she asked him if anything special happened today, he just shrugged his shoulders and shook his head no. He had not had time to really examine the seed which fell on his head in his special hiding place, but he knew it was special. He could not wait until he went back to his special place and have a good look at the seed. At least he had a reason to be anxious to go to school again, although today was Friday. He would not have a chance to sneak back to look at the seed until Monday when he went to school again.

The week-end passed slowly for Eldo because of his anxiousness. When Monday morning arrived, he jumped out of bed and hurriedly dressed for school. His mother had never seen her son so anxious to go to school. When she questioned him what was so special happening today, she just received a shrug of his shoulder. Eldo was bored all day at school; he had more important things to do. The bullies picked on him but his mind was elsewhere and he paid no attention to them. That made them angry. When lunch time came, the bullies took little Eldo's lunch and ate it. Eldo was very hurt and angry but was not big enough to defend himself. He sat in the classroom all afternoon disgusted and angry.

When the school bell finally rang signaling the end of the school day, Eldo ran all the way to his secret hiding place. He wanted to cry but his excitement over the seed kept his tears from flowing. When he crawled into his special place he was met with the most delicious smell. He looked at the spot where he had hid the special seed. Where he had hid the seed was a little tree growing. It was a strange looking tree. Eldo got down on his hands and knees and as he was looking the tree over he just had to smell it. The little tree smelled just like candy. Eldo took very good care of the tree. He watered it and was now even more careful to see he was not followed to his hiding place.

As the little tree grew, each branch formed was different and smelled different. When the tree was four feet tall it started to bloom. Each branch was soon covered with blooms and each branch was different. The blooms soon developed into candy. One branch had candy canes, one had candy kisses, and another branch held brightly colored Christmas candies. When Eldo looked the tree over he also found lollypops, candy bars, chocolate hearts, chocolate Easter eggs, jelly beans, and candy for every occasion. He could not believe what he was seeing. He loved sweets and had to taste candy from each branch. He was not feeling very well when he arrived home. His mother gave him some castor oil, which is supposed to cure all ills and told him to go to bed.

The next day when Eldo arrived at his secret place, he found Elves from the North Pole picking the candy canes and Christmas candy off the tree and putting it in little Christmas sacks. Then they put the filled little Christmas sacks in big red bags. They stopped picking when Eldo arrived and told him they were Santa's helpers. They explained to him the seed had been given to him by a special Christmas angel. Santa had asked her to find someone special to plant the seed and take care of the tree which sprouted from the seed. He needed someone to help him in supplying enough candy canes and Christmas candy for all the children in the world. Santa also said to tell you the other candy was to be picked by you and shared with your classmates and people in need.

Eldo was so proud he had been chosen to help Santa. He was now a Santa helper and was needed. Eldo helped the Christmas Elves pick the rest of the candy canes and Christmas candy. As soon as one piece of candy was picked it was replaced with a bloom. When Santa's Christmas Elves had their big red bags full, they disappeared in a sudden mist. Eldo rubbed his eyes in disbelief. He saw a candy cane and a small Christmas sack of candy lying on the leaves under the tree. He reached down and put the candy cane in his pocket and the little Christmas sack inside of his shirt to eat later.

He sat their for a moment thinking about the little elves who worked for Santa and what they had said. He reached up and plucked a candy kiss off of the candy tree. The new blooms smelled so good. As he ate the candy kiss, he did exactly as the Elves had told him what Santa wanted him to do. When ever there was a birthday in his class he took candy for the classmate to pass out. Lollipops were their favorite. He even took candy for the bullies to pass out on their birthdays. They were surprised and soon changed their opinion of him. They no longer would bully him.

He took his little red wagon and loaded it with candy on holidays to take to people in the hospital. He loved to pull his little red wagon full of candy to the nursing home at the edge of the northern woods town. The senior citizens would all brag about him. The newspaper even wrote a story about his good deeds and put it on the front page. He also delivered candy to the homeless Elves. He took the time to find out where the needy families lived and would sneak up and leave candy on their front porch when they were not home. Some of the homes who had candy delivered on their porch were where some of his classmates lived. In one of the homes one of the bullies lived.

Eldo was brought back to the real world when the teacher gently shook him to wake him up. She had noticed he had been daydreaming as she was reading them a Christmas story about a candy tree. When she touched him, she was suddenly filled with the Christmas spirit as she had never felt before. Something was just not right. She had also noticed the class bullies now left little Eldo alone. Eldo felt something in his pocket. He smiled to himself when he saw it was a candy cane. Yes, his tree is real. He felt inside of his shirt and pulled out the little Christmas sack of candy. He handed it to his teacher and in his little soft shy elf voice wished her.

"Merry Christmas."

MADDIE

As you travel the road of life you sometimes see someone who really gets your undivided attention. There is just something about that individual that makes them very special. When you meet this person they become tucked away in your memory. Then one day right out of the clear blue the special memory of that person will be brought forward. One of these special persons I have tucked away is a special young lady named Maddie.

Maddie first caught my attention as I was working in my yard. I saw her playing in the yard across the street where she was visiting her grandparents Jane and Dan Gomer. I guess what impressed me about this young lady was her radiant smile and sparkling eyes. I was visiting her grandparents a few days later and inquired about this young lady I had seen visiting them. I commented on her smile, which just radiated and her sparkling eyes. She is such an active girl. Jane then informed me that Maddie is a diabetic.

I am a volunteer who visits kindergarten classes and read them stories and share other things I have in my tote bag. When I visited Mrs. Holmes's kindergarten class I found Maddie was a student in this class. One thing I made a practice of was to celebrate each student's birthday. At this time, sweets were authorized to be brought to these events; now only non-sweet items can be given to the students except for certain holidays.

The first time I visited this class to celebrate a birthday, I brought ice cream cups and fresh home made cookies Granny had baked. Mrs. Holmes informed me that Maddie would not be allowed to eat any of this without her mother's permission since she is a diabetic. I felt horrible I had brought these items and Maddie could not have them with her class. I soon found out Maddie's mother is a teacher at this school. She was contacted and gave permission for Maddie to participate in celebrating the birthday. We waited for her and then had a nice birthday party. I cringed every time a birthday was to be celebrated. I soon found out that Maddie was a regular little trooper and took this all in stride just as if it was nothing. I admired her courage and for accepting life as it was dealt in such a happy way.

I really didn't know a lot about diabetes. My wife was told she was a border line diabetic several years ago. She was inflicted with boils and carbuncles at that time. She has kept a close check on her sugar level and has had no further problems since then, although diabetes does run in her family. After this first birthday party in Mrs. Holmes class, I looked in the encyclopedia to see what I could learn. I found there in two different types, one being Diabetes mellitus. This is the most common and occurs when the pancreas does not produce enough of the hormone insulin. The second type is Diabetes insipidus and results when the posterior lobe of the pituitary gland does not function normal.

One day while I was visiting Mrs. Holmes's class after Maddie had graduated from kindergarten and was now in the fifth grade, I mentioned Maddie and how she had so impressed me. I mentioned I would like to write a short story about Maddie. Mrs. Holmes readily agreed and confided to me, Maddie was a special student she had locked away in her memory closet. Mrs. Holmes also commented on how diabetes used to affect just a few children and now in was not uncommon. She felt this subject needed brought to the public's attention. I knew Maddie would be a great example to write about and how she so bravely accepted it as part of her daily life. I asked Mrs. Holmes if she would be willing to write her thoughts and feelings for me about Maddie and she readily agreed.

I did not fully understand and do not know enough about the disease to write about it. I thought the best information I could get would be from those who have had first hand experience with diabetes. I called Maddie's parents, Heather and Daniel Gomer, and asked for their permission to include a story in this book about Maddie. I also asked if they would tell me about their experiences with Maddie and any other information they could give me. They also agreed and volunteered to furnish any information they had and their thoughts. I received the following from them. As a parent myself, it touched my heart and opened my eyes.

Heather's thoughts: Up until about thirteen months of age Maddie had never been sicker than just the sniffles. Around the age of thirteen months she started getting sick with bronchitis and pneumonia back to back. She couldn't seem to knock either one. In July of 1999 she had already been to the doctor twice in two days and didn't seem to be getting any better. What was happening, and we had no idea, was her body was attacking the beta cells in her pancreas as it was fighting the other illnesses she was dealing with. On July 7, 1999, I took her to the doctor because she was dehydrated and just wasn't herself. She had a look about her that was so indescribable. The nurse had seen us sitting in the waiting room and had obviously told the doctor how she looked because we were called up to the front desk and told to take her straight to the hospital that the doctor would meet us there. When we got to the hospital they had a room already waiting for Maddie. They were told that there was a child coming who appeared severely dehydrated and would be admitted. The doctor had ordered a panel of blood work to be done while they were getting her hooked up to her IV and settled in. She was hooked to an IV and started receiving fluid. Before my eyes though, my child was getting worse and worse. She started having trouble breathing and her eyes started to roll back in her head. She was going into a diabetic coma, but we had no idea. As I was yelling for the nurse to come in the doctor came in and ripped out the IV (it was sugar water) and told me my child was a diabetic. Why he ran the blood screen that tested blood sugar he will never know, because he said it wasn't a test that he normally had run on an infant, but he did and thankfully so. We obviously had an angel with us because if he (Dr. John Williams) hadn't run that test and he hadn't had the numbers come back (her blood sugar was over 900) she might not be with us today. They got the IV out and got her started on fluid without sucrose in it and got her started on insulin. They stabilized her and early the next morning we were put in an ambulance and sent to LeBonheur hospital in Memphis where we stayed a week learning all the ins and outs of diabetes. We learned all about nutrition and how to do blood sugar checks and how to administer shots. Maddie adjusted so well with everything (better than us at times I feel). Having a toddler with diabetes is like constantly being on a roller coaster. Her blood sugar went up and down so fast as a roller coaster does. Along with high and low blood sugars also came major mood changes. Again though, Maddie has adjusted beautifully. Looking at her no one would know that she is living with a chronic illness. We have treated her as a child with diabetes not a diabetic. So many people ask, "How do you do it?" Well, we just fit it into our lives and didn't let it rule us. Yes, it brought us down a many days and we still have tough times, but it is part of our life and the Good Lord wouldn't have chosen us to deal with it if He didn't think we could handle it. In December of 2002 (3 months after Logan was born) Maddie was put on an insulin pump. That was a day that definitely changed how we deal with diabetes. Her pump has given her so much more freedom than she ever had. We had from December until the next August to get her and us adjusted to her pump so she would be ready for kindergarten. I still remember bringing Maddie to school to meet her teacher, the school nurse, and a few others who were going to learn (some for the first time) about dealing with a child with diabetes. Some people shy away and don't want the responsibility but Mrs. Holmes jumped in and learned the signs, symptoms, and everything else there was to learn to help Maddie have a great first year of school. Each year we have been blessed to have great teachers for Maddie who have kept an eye on her but if it were not for the school nurse Mrs. Brown, I don't know what I would have done over the past several years. She has been an angel taking care of and watching over Maddie when I couldn't. I hate to put responsibility on anyone else, because she is my child, but Mrs. Brown makes it easy to do my job and not have to worry. When people find out that Maddie is a diabetic they are amazed because I guess they expect her to look different, act different, not to do things she does…I don't quite know what they expect. We have made life for her just as it should be….life as a child. She has been very active in dance (tap and ballet) for 5 years. She also has been active in cheerleading. She tried out and made the cheerleading squad in 4th and 5th grade. She is now also in a tumbling cheer class based out of Jonesboro. As you can see she is very active and we don't let anything hold us back. I honestly think the past 10 years have been harder on myself than on my child because I try to take all the stress out of it for her. I try not to let her see the frustration that goes on at times, and boy are there days when the stress level is high, but that is something she needs to deal with. She needs to be just like every other kid and be able to enjoy life to the fullest. Hopefully with everything we have done and will continue to do, Maddie will live a very happy, healthy, productive life.

After I received the information from Heather and Daniel, I was so impressed that I ask them if they thought Maddie would be willing to tell me her views and feelings. When I received the following from Maddie, I was not surprised because it was what I expected from a young lady with such a happy outlook on life.

Maddie's thoughts: I was diagnosed with diabetes when I was a toddler. Some people want to know how it feels to be a diabetic. I think it feels great to be a diabetic. People think it makes me mad. It makes me happy because it's a part of my life. One thing about being a diabetic has taught me about life is not eating sweets. Too many sweets are not good for people. Sometimes people don't understand and are afraid. I am not afraid and it's not as bad as some people think it might be. The main thing I want people to know about being a diabetic is that I feel good about it and I don't care what people say. I'm just like everybody else who likes many activities. I'm a very active girl. My favorite activity is dancing and cheering.

Mrs. Holmes's thoughts: A great friend, bouncy, talkative, hardworking, joyful, cheerful, loving, trustworthy, caring, compassionate, and persevering---just a few words that come to mind when I think of Maddie Gomer.

I'll never forget the first time that I found out that Maddie would be in my room. I was told that I had been scheduled for a "special" meeting with Heather Gomer and Sandy Brown before school started. Briefly, I was made aware that Heather's little girl, Maddie, was coming to school and she had been diagnosed with diabetes. (The only thing I knew about this disease was that my grandfather had it. But, he was not 5 years old, and he was not someone's baby!) I was scared to death!

But for some odd reason-I was the one picked for this job. And with the Lord's help, I would do the very best job that I could do. Heather had entrusted her baby in my care and I would take care of her.

As I look back now, I almost laugh at myself. I remember the first time I had to check Maddie's sugar level. I was afraid that I would hurt her little finger with that odd finger-poking stick. Maddie helped me through it, just as she did all year long. She would just laugh and say, "Oh Mrs. Holmes, you are so funny!" or, "Mrs. Holmes, do it on this side- the blood comes out faster.

Heather was and is such an awesome mother, and Daniel too!

They were both there whenever possible to make sure that everything went as smoothly as possible. Heather did not give Maddie any "special privileges," she just made sure that all necessary accommodations were taken care of, if necessary.

At party time, Heather made special arrangements so that Maddie's treats were just like the rest of the class---just low in sugar content.

I am totally amazed how she and Daniel did it all. They definitely relied on help of the Lord and worked through all of it together.

Maddie gave me several little angel trinkets through out the year that I still adore. Every time I look at them, I think of that truly special little angel that I was blessed with one year. Maddie always sees the bright side of things and faces each task and endeavor with a smile that will knock you down.

Anyone who has been blessed enough to know and love Maddie has truly been "touched by a little angel." I am honored to have been just a small part of Maddie's life. Maddie's a great inspiration to remind me to smile at everything and keep pushing forward. I cannot wait to see what she holds for the future, not what the future holds for her. Whatever it is, it will be amazing and remarkable, and Maddie!

I will finish this story by saying it has indeed been a pleasure and an eye opener to have our paths cross and to meet this family. What a wonderful world this would be if all the children in this world had Maddie's disposition and positive outlook on life. She is what makes each storm cloud have a silver lining.

THE LADY ON THE FRONT PORCH

LITTLE Sadie was slowly walking to school with her backpack. She was humming a little tune as she stopped ever so often to watch a bug on the sidewalk or other little creatures put on this earth for children to watch. Every school day when she came to a yard surrounded by a neat white picket fence, she would have to touch every picket by the sidewalk. When she would come to the opening in the fence where a sidewalk went into a well kept yard, she would wave to a lady sitting on a porch swing watching her. When Sadie waved, the lady would smile and wave back. Then Sadie would continue her stroll to school as she looked for anything that may catch her inquisitive eyes.

When school was out in the afternoon, Sadie would slowly walk home. Sometimes she may be wearing her backpack and other time she would drag it. She would always wave at the little old lady swinging on the porch. She seemed to be waiting everyday for Sadie to walk by. One day Sadie stopped by the opening in the fence as she smiled and waved to the lady. The lady said.

"What is your name young lady? You are such a busy young lady."

Sadie replied.

"My name is Sadie and I can not come in your yard because my mom told me I can wave to you and speak but I can not go into your yard and bother you. My mom told me you are Mrs. Shelby, she knows you."

The lady smiled and replied.

"Sadie you will not bother me. I love company like you."

Sadie smiled as she turned to continue her journey home. She would tell her mom she had spoken to the lady on the porch and she liked her. When Sadie arrived home she deposited her backpack on a kitchen chair for her mother to inspect. She climbed up on another chair where a peanut butter and jelly sandwich was waiting for her with a glass of milk on the table. With a mouthful of sandwich she tried to tell her mother she had stopped and spoken to Mrs. Shelby, but had not gone into her yard. She also told her that she liked Mrs. Shelby. Sadie's mother smiled as her daughter talked while she examined the contents of the backpack. She found a happy face on her papers and also another paper requiring homework. Her mother put it on the table as she said.

"Sadie, you can go out to play as soon as you finish your homework. There is no better time to do it than now."

Sadie knew it would do no good to argue. She finished her sandwich and then went to work on her homework with her mother by her side. When she finished her homework, she put on her play clothes and out the back door she went. It was time to visit her dog and tell him about her day.

The next day on her way to school she waved to Mrs. Shelby. Mrs. Shelby waved back and said.

"Good morning Sadie, I hope you have a great day."

When school was out for the day, Sadie took her time walking home as she examined the world around her. When she came to Mrs. Shelby home she found her sitting on the front porch swing. Sadie stopped in front of her yard and then took one step into the front yard. She smiled and waved as she kept one hand on the picket fence. The next day she took two steps into the front yard and could not reach the picket fence. Each day as she was going home after school she would take another step as she talked to Mrs. Shelby. After she had reached the half way point across the front yard she asked her mother if it was alright to talk to Mrs. Shelby on her way home from school.

Her mother said.

"Yes you can visit with her but don't become a bother to her. She is a nice lady."

Within two weeks Sadie had crossed the front yard one step at a time and found a seat on the front steps to Mrs. Shelby's porch. She really liked talking to Mrs. Shelby. Mrs. Shelby soon knew all about Sadie's dog and all her classmates. One day Sadie asked Mrs. Shelby.

"Why does your house have a place for you to sit outside and mine don't?"

Mrs. Shelby smiled and replied.

"Sadie where we are sitting is called a front porch. This is an older home and yours is new. Where your house is located I used to play games. It was a field and a farmer raised his crops there. When I was your age we did not have television or air conditioning. We didn't even have electricity. We used the front porch for our air conditioning; sometimes we even slept on the porch. We used it for our television too. We would sit on the porch every evening and visit with our neighbors just like you and I are doing now. We watched the sun as it disappeared over the horizon as we listened to the bugs chirp and the birds sing. This was our place for entertainment. People now have television, air conditioning and they no longer build porches on houses. People no longer even visit with their neighbors. Sadie, I would rather have my front porch and people to watch and visit with than all the televisions and air conditioners in this world. If I didn't have my front porch I would never have met you."

Sadie stepped upon the porch and climbed up in the swing beside Mrs. Shelby. She looked into Mrs. Shelby's eyes as she said.

"I am glad you have a front porch, too. Someday I am going to have a front porch."

YARD TRASH TO SCHOOL TREASURES

FALL was in the air and a kindergarten teacher knew her class would rather be outside enjoying the nice weather. Soon winter would be here and they would not get to go outside as often. The leaves were starting to dance in the air as they drifted to the ground. When they were on the ground the wind could and would really make them dance. Once they settled down with other leaves they would start the slow process to become nourishment for the trees. Acorns and hickory nut were also falling and hiding among the leaves.

The teacher gave each student a plastic bag she had saved when she had bought her groceries. She then told the class to put on their coats and hats. They were going to go on a nature excursion. She saw a look of puzzlement on her kindergarten student faces. She explained excursion that sounds like a big word, but it means a little sight seeing trip. When her students had their coats and hats on, she had them line up at the door. She put one finger by her lips and said.

"We must be real quiet. The other classes must not hear us since we are taking a special trip outside."

The children followed their teacher down the hall and out the door as quiet as an excited class of kindergarten children can be. The teacher had the children follow her to a near by yard where different types of trees grew. She told her students to pick up anything they found interesting laying on the ground such as acorns, hickory nuts, or colored leaves. They could even pick up tiny rocks, twigs, or just whatever caught their attention.

As the children were searching for yard trash, the teacher was taking individual pictures of her students. Of course, the students got to sit in a circle and play a game of drop an acorn instead of a hanky. They then returned to searching for trash in the yard and chasing the dancing leaves as they fell from the trees. It turned out to be a fun way to study nature and pick up fall trash in a yard. When they all had an ample supply of trash in their used grocery sacks, they lined up and again followed their teacher. They followed their teacher to a dumpster, outside of the lunch room. At the dumpster, they watched their teacher take two clean, big flattened cardboard boxes out. She then told the class the excursion was now over and it was time to quietly return to the classroom where they would turn the yard trash into a treasure.

When they arrived back into the classroom, each row took their turn getting a much needed drink of water and of course the ladies in each row got to have their turn first. Then the important work began as they watched their teacher cut a picture frame for each student from the cardboard boxes she had collected. When the cardboard picture frames were cut out she had each student take their favorite trash from their used plastic sack she had given them to collect their trash in.

She told the class to take their glue and glue onto the picture frame the trash they wanted on it. The students were amazed as they watched their yard trash become kindergarten classroom treasures. When each student had completed their gluing project under the guidance of their teacher, they saw freshly glued on the frame of the cardboard acorns, twigs, little rocks, colored leaves, and an occasional unidentified object. The teacher had them go one at a time and place their little picture frame on a table to dry overnight.

As the picture frames were drying, the teacher gave each student a sheet of white paper. She had them take a fall colored leaf they had collected and place it on the paper off to one side. She then had them fold the sheet of paper over the leaf like a sandwich. Then she showed them how to take a pencil and lightly scribble the folded paper over the leaf where it would show the leaf design. The class was amazed when they saw the outline of the leaf with ribs in dark pencil and the thin web part of the leaf was light. They each took their pencil and following her instructions made the leaf inside the paper suddenly appear on the outside of the paper.

The next day the cardboard picture frames were spray painted the colors of fall. The teacher had taken her digital camera to a store after school the evening before and had prints made of each student as they searched for their yard treasures. The teacher took the pictures she had taken of her class and put each student's picture in their own yard trash picture frame where it would become a treasured possession of each student for their parents.

Before the class took their nature picture frames home, they were displayed outside of their classroom. They fit right in with the fall season subject matter they had been studying. They had recycled yard trash into a classroom treasure and had learned that it wasn't yard trash after all but another one of Mother Nature's decorations. The picture would become a treasured memory of the day they took a fall kindergarten classroom excursion.

WHISKERS

GRAMPS was visiting a kindergarten class and reading them a story about a kitten. When he read to the class about the kitten washing its' face and whiskers after drinking milk, one student raised his hand and wanted to know what whiskers are. Gramps explained it is the long projecting hairs or bristles growing near the mouth of an animal such as a cat or dog. He should have stopped there and continued on with the story, but he continued on explaining that mustaches and beards are a collection of whiskers. Whiskers are bristles on the face like your daddy has on his face and you can feel when he holds your face close to his. My dad would scratch my face with his whiskers and make my skin burn.

A wave of hands could be seen waving in the air as every student had something to add. One young lady seemed to be overly excited so Gramps let her stand up and have her say. She said.

"My Grandma has whiskers; she tries to pull them out with tweezers and gets big tears in her eyes. Sometimes she puts stuff on them to make them go away. One time I saw her use my Grandpa's electric razor. They grow on her top lip like a man's mustache. She has a long hair growing out of a dark spot on her face too. I pulled it one time but it was stuck hard; she scolded me."

With all the students waving their hands in the air, Gramps decided to let each one have their say. The next student had to tell about his mom shaving under her arms. He continued on that his dad doesn't shave under his arms and his mom tells him that it looks like a rat's nest.

Gramps knew he was in for some interesting stories. The next student was a young lady who told how she had cut her dog's whiskers off with her school scissors. Her dad said.

"You should not cut off the whiskers of a dog or cat. Those whiskers are their feelers. They use them for feeling."

She then proceeded to tell about an old man that has a long hair growing out of the top of his ear. He sits in front of her family in church and she watches it every Sunday to see how long it gets. She whispered to her mom one day in church.

"Does he have that long feeler whisker on his ear so he can feel what he is hearing?"

Her brother laughed out loud and she was told to be quiet.

Her little story made more hands wave in the air.

Another little girl then told of a neighbor lady that has a long black feeler whisker growing on her nose.

A little boy sitting in the front row then pointed out to the class that Gramps has a long whisker on top of his ear. Gramps felt and sure enough he did have a hair sticking up. He would have to cut it when he got home.

All of the kindergarten class was giggling as they each told their story. Gramps was enjoying their little stories but was also wishing he had not started this story telling. He was afraid the teacher may not like it, but he had noticed the stories had brought a sparkle to her eyes.

A little boy had to tell about a mouse his dad had caught in a mouse trap. He went on to describe how its' eyes bugged out and it had whiskers. His dad had put peanut butter on the trap and the mouse had some peanut butter on its' whiskers. Gramps smiled as he could just imagine how the young lad had closely inspected the mouse in the trap.

What really surprised Gramps was when a young lady in the class then told about a mouse her mom had caught in a mouse trap. She told how it looked with its' eyes open. She then informed the class how her cat ate the mouse. She said.

"Gramps, do you know they eat the mouse and the tail sticks out of the cat's mouth last?"

All the girls in the class responded with an.

"Ooooooh, nasty!"

Gramps noticed several of the students verified her story on how cats eat mice; it seems like children take the time to notice tiny details like that. Gramps went on to think to himself.

"Children notice a lot of details and are willing to share what they have seen."

Gramps was trying to bring the subject to a close, but one young lady was all wiggly and had a story that just must be told. She said.

"My mom gets whiskers on her chin. She can feel them with her finger. She takes tweezers and tries to pull them out. She tells my dad. "Those whiskers just drive me crazy!" I hope I don't get whiskers when I grow up."

When all of the class had volunteered their stories about whiskers,

Gramps finished the story he had been reading to the class. When he finished he packed up his bags he had brought to the class and bid the class, "Good by." He knew he had better cut that long whisker on his ear when he arrived home because the class would be looking for it when he came back to read to them again.

GRANDMA'S FULL-LENGTH MIRROR

LITTLE Katie loved to go visit her grandma and listen to her stories about the old, veneer, full-length mirror in the entrance hall. Katie always had to stop and admire herself in the mirror when she went to see Grandma. Grandma had told her.

"The mirror has stored in it the reflections of everyone who has taken the time to pause and look in it."

Katie had seen her grandma take the time to check herself for proper dress whenever she went out into the public. She especially took the extra time when she was going to church. She would gently pat her hair and straighten her hat. Then she would put on her coat and check it for straightness and lint. When she was through checking the front she would turn and check the hem on her dress. She was very careful about her slip not showing. Katie would stand and watch as her grandma went through her routine.

When Grandma was through, Little Katie took her turn in front of the mirror. She would lean in close and try to peek into the mirror and see those whose reflections would be inside watching her. She tried to see off to the side on the inside but never saw anyone hiding there unless she wanted to.

When Grandma would see Katie sitting in front of the mirror with her doll and talking to someone she would ask Katie.

"Who are you talking to?"

Katie would always have an answer. It may be her grandpa, or her dolly. One time she told Grandma she was visiting with Grandpa's old hunting hound. Katie had even visited with Santa Claus because she knew Santa had looked in the mirror when he delivered presents. One time she told Grandma.

"I saw Grandpa's old hunting hound chasing the Easter Bunny but he couldn't catch him."

Katie also told her grandma.

"You know you can step into the mirror and go any place you want to. You never come to the end of anything when you are inside the mirror. I have looked hard and can't see how far it goes. I have seen a lot of people in the mirror though. One time I saw Grandpa and we fished like we used to. I have even seen my dad when he was a little boy. He didn't know me then but I told him he would someday. Grandma, I even have seen you in the mirror and visited with you. One time you gave me one of your little hankies you carry in your purse on Sunday."

Grandma smiled as she asked her granddaughter.

"Would you like to have one of my little handkerchiefs?"

Katie jumped up and quickly answered.

"Yes!"

Grandma went into the bedroom and took a freshly pressed hanky out of a drawer. She gave it to her granddaughter in front of the mirror so the mirror would always remember when Katie got it.

One evening when Katie was visiting her grandma and was going to stay with her for the night, she crawled upon her Grandma's lap and asked her.

"Do you think I can have the tall mirror in the hall when you no longer need it?"

Grandma smiled and hugged her and said.

"I don't see why you can't have it. I would like to know why you want that old mirror though."

Katie replied.

"Remember you told me that everyone who has looked in the mirror is in there with their reflection. I know my grandpa and daddy are in there. I would just step inside the mirror and visit with them. I would visit with you too Grandma."

Grandma gave Katie a tender hug and kiss. She then replied.

"Katie, someday if you still want the mirror you can have it. All I ask is that you take good care of it and Grandpa."

The following year Grandma became ill and was hospitalized. While in the hospital she told her son.

"Katie asked me if she could have the full-length mirror in the front hallway when I don't need it anymore. It means so much to her. You know it was my mothers. She received it as a wedding present. Katie thinks she can visit with everyone who has taken the time to look into the mirror. She has even visited with you when you were a little boy. She said you didn't know her but you would someday."

The following day Katie's dad took the old mirror from the hallway and took it home to Katie. Katie wanted it put in her bedroom.

Everyday Katie would take a trip into the mirror and visit. She made a special effort to find Grandma in the mirror and help take care of her. It wasn't long before Grandma recovered and was visiting with Katie in front of the mirror. The mirror remembered all the conversations and would tell them again to Katie someday.

Katie even met her great grandma in the mirror and seen her grandma when she was a little girl. She gave her doll to Grandma because she never had one that nice when she was a young girl. The dolls she had were all home made.

When Grandma left to be with Grandpa, Katie found so much comfort in the mirror. She was positive she saw Grandma inside the mirror watching her the day she tried on her wedding dress. On Katie's wedding day, she stood in front of the mirror and gently patted her hair just like Grandma used to pat her hair before she went to church. Katie then tenderly touched her grandma's face in the mirror. She knew Grandma would always be in the mirror to guide her through life and give her advice.

A GIFT IN RETURN

Mrs. Linda Holmes and Mrs. Karen Sullivan made plans to have their students bring gifts to school to be given to foster children. Santa and Rufus the oldest elf at the North Pole were listening in on their plans. Their classes have the following students.

Mrs. Linda Holmes class	Mrs. Karen Sullivan class
Gracie	Hannah
Benny	Kalob
Rusty	Leah
Cameron	Joseph (J.J.)
Brayden	Cannon
Logan	Garrett
Joshua C.	Riyanna
Emily	Erin
Lindsay	Akiria
Quavaun	Gabby
Maycie	Skyler
Haley	Tucker

Kezaireous	Shelby
Lauren	Darcie
Aaliyah	Tyler
Scott	Xavier
Alexa	Jacob (J.D.)
Billy	Devon
Druw	Amaury
J'Kyris	

Santa and Rufus listened with interest as the two teachers made plans to send notes home with each student requesting a gift from each to be given to less fortunate children. The teachers planned to ask the school for permission to have a school bus take the classes along with their gifts to the bank where the Christmas gifts would be collected for delivery to the needy children. Over the next three week Santa and Rufus watched as a Christmas tree was placed in each classroom by the teachers and decorated by the students under the watchful eyes of their teachers.

The notes were made and sent home with each student. The response was overwhelming. The floor under the Christmas tree in each room was soon covered with presents. Santa and Rufus were amazed at the generosity of the parents and the children. Santa told Rufus.

"Rufus, we need to give these children and their teachers a gift in return. I have an idea; what do you think about rigging the big cargo sleigh with electro-magnetic metal runners and after the children deliver their presents and are on the way back to the school, you and I along with some elf helpers will land the cargo sleigh on the bus? We will turn on the electromagnets on the runners and pick the bus up. We will fly it with the reindeer and cargo sleigh up here to the North Pole and give the children a tour of Toyland and the Northern Lights.

I would love to meet this generous class and I know Mrs. Claus would be very pleased to have company."

Rufus slapped his little knee and laughed as he replied.

"Santa, you are always coming up with great ideas. I just know we can modify the cargo sleigh and have it ready to carry out your idea. I will have the helpers also get the enclosed rainbow stairway ready so we can put it between the sleigh and the bus."

Santa replied with a sparkle in his eyes and his jolly voice.

"I like the idea of the rainbow stairway. I will talk to our retired elf school teacher, "Elizabeth," and have her visit with Mrs. Holmes and Mrs. Sullivan to inform them of our plan. We will need the school and each parent's permission for this trip."

Mrs. Holmes and Mrs. Sullivan were highly pleased with the gift response they received for the foster children program. They had asked the principal for permission to have a school bus take their classes to the bank in a nearby city where the gifts were being collected for distribution. Mrs. Middleton, the principal readily approved their request. They were discussing their final plans one day while the children were on the playground following their lunch period when a small lady elf appeared. She introduced herself as Elizabeth, a retired elf school teacher from the North Pole and stated Santa had sent her to visit with them.

She told them.

"Santa and an old elf named Rufus have been eavesdropping on you as you made plans for collecting gifts for the foster children program. They had watched and listened as the children responded to your request for gifts in an unselfish manner. Santa wants to give them a gift in return by taking them to visit the North Pole. He has sent me to see if you could get the school and parents permission for this trip. There will be no expense to anyone. Santa's plan is to pick up your bus with his cargo sleigh as you are returning from delivering the gifts and fly you to the North Pole where you and the children will be his guest for a week-end. Santa also is aware that Gramps reads to your classes. He would like for him to accompany your classes to the North Pole so the two of them can reminisce over old times. Elizabeth also asked the teachers to inform the bus driver about the trip and what to expect. Santa did not want to surprise the driver while driving the bus."

The two teachers could not believe what was happening. They were kind of skeptical to agree to such a plan but after a short discussion agreed to the plan and would try to get the permission Santa needed and required. After visiting with the North Pole elf lady named Elizabeth, they did believe what Elizabeth had told them. When Elizabeth heard the children coming down the hall from the playground, she bid the teachers good-by and disappeared in a small fog cloud.

The teachers talked to the principal and told her of the visit they had with the retired elf school teacher from the North Pole. Mrs. Middleton smiled as she gave the trip her blessings. She had been to the North Pole and visited with Mr. and Mrs. Claus so she knew their trip would actually happen if the parents gave their permission. She knew she would be returning to the North Pole with two other classes on a train called Little Toot.

Both teachers sent permission slips home with the children and received all of them back approved. They also told Gramps of the conversation with an elf name Elizabeth. Gramps readily agreed to ride with the classes when the presents were delivered and was sure Granny and he would also have gifts for the foster children. Excitement grew everyday in the classrooms as the time to deliver the gifts came closer day by day. The student's time was also occupied as they practiced for their Christmas program. The teachers had planned to deliver the presents to the foster children on a Friday. This would be the day after their Christmas program.

The children's parents attended the Christmas program the two classes performed together. Unknown to the students or their teachers, Santa and Rufus were watching and listening to the program. They were as excited as the children and looking forward for the time to arrive when the gifts were delivered and the bus then would be picked up. Santa planned to use his large work reindeer for this mission. They are Brutus, Claude, Cletus, Ethyl, George, Ralph, Rosie and Sam. He would need this large reindeer team for their pulling power. He kept his special reindeer team to deliver presents on Christmas Eve. They were lighter and faster. They could land on a roof and do no damage. He could just imagine what would happen if he tried to land his large work team on a roof.

The next day as the children were going into their classroom, Santa and his helpers were harnessing the reindeer work team and hitching them to the special cargo sleigh with the electromagnet runners. When they were hitched to the sleigh, Santa walked to his house and as he hugged his wife good-by he said.

"When I return, I will bring you some very special company."

Mrs. Claus replied.

"I will be anxiously waiting. The elf families have made all the arrangements for the children to stay with them and the teachers and bus driver will stay with us. We'll make Gramps sleep in the reindeer barn. We'll have a hot meal waiting for them."

Santa chuckled because he knew Gramps would not have to sleep in the barn, although he planned to visit with him a lot there. Santa stepped outside and pulled his red cap down over his ears. When he got back to the barn, all the helper elves that were scheduled to go on this special trip were aboard the sleigh. Rufus was sitting in the driver's seat holding the reins and talking gently to the reindeer team. Santa crawled up in the sleigh beside Rufus and said.

"Turn them loose Rufus; we have a special cargo to pick up and bring back here."

Rufus nodded his head and as he loosened the reins yelled.

"Go Brutus, go Claude and Cletus and Ethyl, go George and Ralph and Rosie and Sam. Up, up, and away."

The work team responded and soon snow was flying and then they lifted off into the cold crisp air lit up by the northern lights. Rufus turned them in a southern direction. The helper elves double checked all the supplies they had loaded and made sure the rainbow stairway was secured.

As Santa and his elf helpers were streaking through the sky, Mrs. Holmes and Mrs. Sullivan were having their students putting on their hat and coats. When they were all bundled up, they each picked up the gift they had brought to school for the foster children. They lined up in single file and walked out to a waiting school bus. Gramps put all the remaining presents into two large Christmas bags and followed the classes to the bus. When all were aboard and safely seated, the bus pulled out and started an unforgettable trip.

The school bus soon pulled into a bank parking lot and the children carried their gifts into the bank and put them into a very large box. Two ladies, who were the organizers for this gift drive, welcomed the two classes. A reporter from the local newspaper took pictures of the class as they sang a Christmas carol. Gramps deposited the remaining gifts into another large box and then it was time to go back to school. They lined up and walked back to the bus. Each teacher was so very proud of her class. They had conducted themselves like ladies and gentlemen and each gift delivered had come from their heart. When all were seated back on the bus, the bus driver pulled out of the parking lot and headed the bus back toward the school. The children were singing Christmas carols they had sung in their program. Just after they had passed the city limits and gained speed after turning onto the highway, all aboard the bus heard a clunk on top of the bus and then they heard.

"Up, up and away you reindeer. Go Brutus, go Claude, go Cletus and Ethyl, go George, Ralph, Rosie and Sam."

As the children looked out of the bus windows they saw the ground falling away from them. When they looked out of the windshield of the bus they could see a team of reindeer flying in front of them. The teachers assured the children that all was well. Santa had the elf helpers remove the enclosed rainbow stairway from its storage place and installed it between the sleigh and the bus door. When all was secure, Santa walked down the steps and into the bus. As he stepped into the bus he said.

"Ho, ho, ho, these two classes have been so generous giving the gifts they just delivered. I thought you deserved a gift in return. We are now headed toward the North Pole where all of you will be Mrs. Claus and my guest for the week-end. During your visit the children will be staying with the elf helper families and the rest will stay with Mrs. Claus and me. We have a rainbow stairway which is enclosed so those of you who wish to visit the sleigh and help Rufus and me drive the reindeer team will be welcome too. The helper elves are bringing food and drink for you to enjoy and will furnish entertainment to make your trip enjoyable.

As the children watched in amazement, five elf helpers entered the bus carrying arctic clothing for the teachers and students to put on. They were entering cold air as they climbed into the sky as they journeyed north. After all were warmly dressed, three lady elves handed out pizza and soft drinks. The teachers and those who would rather have hot cocoa and sandwiches were served those. As the classes ate their lunch, they looked out of the windows and watched the ground below. They not only saw the scenery change to a snow covered terrain but also could see the lakes and river covered with ice. After watching the scenery below, the students wanted to walk up the stairway and see the reindeer and sleigh. Rufus and Gramps led five students at a time as Santa drove the reindeer. Benny, Rusty, Cameron, Braydon and Logan were the first to climb the stairs and help Santa drive the reindeer. They were followed by Joshua C., Quavaun, Kezaireous, Scott and Billy. Druw, J,Kyris, Kalob, Joseph (J.J.), and Garrett soon were in the sleigh and each had a turn holding the reins. When they returned to the bus, Devon, Jacob (J.D.), Xavier, Tyler and Tucker had their turn.

The rest of the class waited until they had finished their lunch. As they were entering the Northern Lights or also known as the Aurora Borealis, Gracie, Emily, Lindsay, Maycie, Haley, Lauren, Aaliyah, Amaury, and Alexa climbed the stairway. They were entranced with the beauty they saw in the heavens. After they re-entered the bus, Hannah, Leah, Riyanna, Erin, Akiria, Gabby, Skyler, Shelby, and Darcie climbed the stairway and could not believe the sight they were seeing. They watched Santa and the reindeer as they rode through the lights. They each took a turn holding onto the reins. Finally, it was time for them to return to the bus as Santa had the North Pole in sight and was starting a slow approach.

He handed the reins to Rufus and as they approached to land. Santa went to the bus and told the bus driver to hold the bus wheels straight and when they touched down the bus would be released from the sleigh. Santa then returned to the sleigh for the landing. The helper elves removed the enclosed rainbow stairway and stowed it on the sleigh. Santa made a perfect approach and a soft landing. Just as the bus touched down, Santa released the bus and guided his reindeer to land beside it. They came to a stop by the sleigh garage. Some helper elves were waiting and opened the door so the bus and sleigh could enter the warm building. After all were parked in the garage, Santa and Rufus had the teachers and children get off of the bus and then escorted them to Santa's house.

Mrs. Claus was beside herself when she was introduced to the teachers, bus driver and children. She gave each and everyone of them a hug including Gramps. Mrs. Claus and some of the elf ladies had prepared a hot meal for everyone. Mrs. Claus knew the children would be tired and hungry. Santa said the blessing and then helped make the meal disappear. After all the children had finished their dessert, they were escorted to the elf's home where they were to be their guest for the week-end. The children were amazed to find all the furniture in the elf home was just the perfect size for them. They all wished they had furniture like that in their own bedrooms. The children spent the evening getting acquainted with the families they were staying with.

Mrs. Claus and the ladies were visiting over a cup of hot chocolate and homemade cookies. Santa and Gramps had disappeared into the barn after the evening meal and were feeding the work reindeer and brushing them after their hard pull. Santa was very proud of all of his reindeer. When they finished they sat down on a bale of hay and caught up on the news since they had seen each other last year. After a busy day, the lights in every house were soon turned off and everyone rested without stirring.

Everyone woke up early and was anxious to meet the new day. The children ate a hearty breakfast with the elf families while everyone else ate with Santa and Mrs. Claus. Santa sure loved his biscuits and gravy and could make them disappear quickly. Gramps noticed Santa always got a little gravy on his beard and would take his big red handkerchief and wipe the gravy off. Santa and Mrs. Claus enjoyed their visitors very much and were anxious to hear what everyone had to say. After breakfast the ladies done the dishes and then had another cup of coffee and visited before they made the beds. Santa and Gramps met all the students in Toyland and took them on a tour of the huge toy factory. They would spend their day inspecting all the items and were never able to find what they liked best. They wanted and liked everything. The girls liked the doll section and were surprised at the variety of dolls on the shelves ready to be wrapped and packaged for delivery on Christmas Eve. The boys enjoyed the toy truck section but when they came to the four-wheeler section, they all had to sit upon them and pretend they were going 100 miles per hour.

While they were visiting Toyland, they were each given a chance to go for a ride on snowmobiles with Santa and Rufus. Some of the children tried their luck at ice skating. They each were given a new pair of boot skates. This was the first time any of them had every rode on a snowmobile or tried to ice skate. Santa chuckled as he watched them fall as they tried to skate. He knew they would all be sore from their falls when they went to bed that night.

Santa showed the children all the new video games and let them each play some. Gramps didn't play with any. He would not admit it was all strange to him and he would never learn how to play them. He knew all the students were smarter than him when it came to video games. At noon, the children were ready for another hot meal. They all had a huge appetite from all the fresh air. Every one of the children enjoyed watching Santa make food disappear except for what he left on his beard. They readily saw he had a huge appetite. He also loved his desserts and could never stop with just one piece of pie. He always had a twinkle in his eye when Mrs. Claus would pretend to scold him over how much he ate. He would just rub his fat tummy and loosen his big wide black belt.

After dinner was through, the teachers and students were taken to Toyland where they would spend their time trying to see and do everything. Santa and Gramps made the excuse they had to feed and check on the reindeer in the barn. They did check on the deer and then they lay in the hay and each had a good snooze. The ladies all pitched in with the elf ladies and washed the dishes. Mrs. Claus did not have a dishwasher. She didn't think she needed one for just Santa and her. After the dishes were all put away and the kitchen straightened, the lady elves went to their houses. They would feed the children who were staying with them their evening meal.

After Santa and Gramps woke up from their naps, they went to

Toyland to check on the children. When they arrived they found the children in every section watching and helping the elf workers make toys and fill Christmas orders. The teachers went back to the Claus house and spent the rest of the afternoon visiting with Mrs. Claus. Santa let the children ride bicycles, battery powered four wheelers, little motor scooter and a miniature rocket ship. The children were kept busy all afternoon trying to see and do everything. They could not believe that there were toys and electronic games they had never seen before.

It was supper time too soon for most of the students. The time had passed so quickly. After everyone had eaten their fill of their favorite food, they all met at the North Pole Community Center. The children performed their Christmas program for Santa and Mrs. Claus plus all the elf families. They were soon joined in their singing by the elf children. Even Santa had to get up and sing with the children. After the program was over, everyone joined in fun and games. They made candy, bobbed for apples and ate homemade ice cream and cookies. Santa let all the children know that eating ice cream and cookies was his favorite time.

The next morning they all gathered in the North Pole Community Center for breakfast together. After all were seated, Santa said the blessing. Santa then had his usual biscuits and gravy. The children quit counting after he had eaten six biscuits and had a lot of gravy on his beard. He never wiped his beard with his big red handkerchief until he was through eating. To do it before he believed was a waste of time. The children had their choice of pancakes and syrup, donuts, French toast, eggs, bacon, sausage, ham, hot cereal and cold cereal. They all had a hard time deciding what they wanted to eat.

After breakfast, the children were all escorted to the barn where they could play in the hay loft or help feed and pet the reindeer. Santa had a long hay rope tied to the barn rafters so the children could swing high and drop on the hay below. Of course, he had to show them how to do it. The children all laughed when they saw Santa do a cannon ball off of the end of the hay rope. The children were especially surprised to find out Santa had an old hound dog with long ears in the barn. Santa told them his name is, "Clarence." It was hard for Gramps to tell who enjoyed the other the most, Clarence or the children. Clarence just about wagged his tail off from being petted and the children about wore their grinner out.

Santa had his elf helpers saddle an old retired gentle reindeer. The children were then all given a short ride on the old reindeer. While some were riding the reindeer, Rufus had harnessed two reindeer and hitched them to a bob sled. He gave children rides as they sang, "Jingle Bells." Mrs. Holmes and Mrs. Sullivan also had a turn riding with the children on the bob sled but refused the offer to ride the old reindeer. They both did swing on the hay rope up in the hay loft.

It was soon time to eat dinner and then pack up to go home. They all returned to the community center where lunch was ready and waiting. Santa again said the blessing.

"As we eat this hot meal
before we get on our way,
bless this food and children
with all my heart I pray.
I pray for their safety,
and may You guide my sleigh
as we return this precious cargo
to where they now stay.
They have been so generous to others
they found in need.
I am so grateful,
for their generous deed.
May in their unselfish hearts
they will always find
the satisfaction of giving

will give them peace of mind.
and may they always be
remembered for the unselfish influence
they've shown to You and me.
Amen."

After Santa had eaten his usual large dinner, he belched ever so slightly as he wiped his whiskers with his red handkerchief. He stood up and asked his helpers to meet him in the barn and help him harness the worker reindeer for the return trip. The teachers asked their students to gather their personal belonging and pack them for the trip home. They would be leaving as soon as Santa and his helpers had the sleigh ready. After the work reindeer were harnessed, they were led over to the sleigh garage where other helper elves had the sleigh and bus ready to travel.

Everyone gathered in the sleigh garage for their farewells. Mrs. Claus shed tears as she hugged every student and both teachers. She thanked them for being such wonderful guest. As the children boarded the bus their teachers had them thank the elf families for the generous hospitality. Santa told the bus driver.

"When all the children are seated, start your bus. After it is warm pull out of the garage and follow the path in the snow we used when we landed. Get up as much speed as you can and we will pick the bus up with the sleigh like we did on the trip before. After we are airborne, the elves will attach the enclosed rainbow stairway so we can visit on the trip. Good luck."

Santa climbed aboard the sleigh and Rufus handed him the reins. The helper elves gave one last inspection to make sure the stairway was secured and all the needed supplies were aboard. Santa watched as the bus driver started the bus and let it idle for a while to warm up. He followed the bus with his work reindeer team and sleigh as it pulled out of the garage. He could hear the children singing Christmas carols and saw Mrs. Claus waving her apron as they gained speed. He knew she was crying. When the bus speed was ample, Santa yelled.

"Go Brutus and Claude. Go Cletus and Ethyl. Go George and Ralph and Rosie and Sam, too. Up, up and away you deer."

The reindeer team climbed into the air and Santa guided the sleigh over the bus where he settled down ever so gentle on it and Rufus turned on the electromagnet. When the bus was secured, Santa spoke again to his reindeer team and they climbed up into the swirling Northern Lights as they made a slow turn in a southern direction. After they had gained altitude, the elves attached the enclosed stairway between the sleigh and the bus door. Santa handed the reins to Rufus and climbed down the steps to visit with the children. He had a red sack slung over his shoulder and a gift bag for each student in it.

He entered the bus with a merry Ho-Ho-Ho and strolled down the aisle giving each one a present. He took the time for each one to tell him what they wanted for Christmas. He visited with Mrs. Holmes and Mrs. Sullivan also. He gave them a gift and praised them for having such a well-mannered class. He also let them know how proud he was of them for the time they had taken with their students to help the Foster children.

The elf ladies entered the bus with snacks and drinks for everyone. Santa stayed while the lunch was consumed. He then told the bus driver.

"When we get back to the school, we will approach the school from the north and have the bus land on the highway. We will release the bus upon touchdown and you can then drive back to the elementary school where the parents will be waiting. Dusk will just be settling in so we will make one pass over the Christmas light display, "Lights of the Delta," for the children to see from the air. Remember to keep your wheels straight on touchdown and thank you for volunteering your time."

After Santa returned to the sleigh, the children again took turns climbing the enclosed staircase and riding in the sleigh with Santa. They enjoyed the view as snow covered mountains and frozen lakes passed below. They even got to take the reins and guide the reindeer on their trek south. Santa enjoyed the company. He told them about Clarence riding with him for company as he delivered Christmas presents. Clarence loved to feel the wind as it flapped his ears. Santa also pointed out the stars he used to find his way around the world.

Santa gave each student a hug and bid each student a Merry Christmas as they left to climb down the steps to the bus. Gramps stayed and visited with Santa until the school was in sight. As they circled the, "Lights of the Delta," Gramps bid Santa, Rufus and the helper elves good-by. After he was safely aboard the bus, the helper elves removed the enclosed stairway. After circling, Santa lined up with the highway and gently deposited the bus down on the blacktop. Rufus hit the release switch and Santa spoke to his work reindeer and they swiftly climbed into the evening sky as they headed back to the North Pole.

The bus driver slowed the bus and turned onto the school property. The children's parents were all anxiously waiting for the precious cargo that was aboard the yellow school bus. It was a trip the children would never forget and they had truly received, "A GIFT IN RETURN," from Santa.

VOICES IN THE TREES

LITTLE Jake was visiting his Grandpa and eyeing the giant oak tree in the backyard as he sat on the back step petting Pete the old cattle dog. He turned and saw his Grandpa asleep in an old beat up rocking chair. He had heard him snoring as he eyed the tree. He got up off of the step and walked over to where his Grandpa was sleeping. He paused for a moment before he decided to wake him up. He had a question that just needed answered and he could not wait any longer. He tugged at Grandpa's shirt sleeve and watched as one eye opened ever so slowly. He said.

"Grandpa, do you think I can climb that big tree, as he pointed to the giant old oak?"

Grandpa slowly opened the other eye and replied.

"Jake, I sure don't know why you can't. You know your daddy used to climb that tree and so did I when I was just a young whippersnapper like you. If you listen closely, you will be able to hear voices in the tree. Some of the voices are tree angels and they sing about the four seasons as the wind blows through the branches. The tree has a way of talking to whoever will take the time to listen. That old tree used to tell me all about its' past. Oak trees can live from 200 to 300 years.

One of the oldest trees measures 27 feet across its trunk and can reach 150 feet into the sky. You know the tree remembers the Civil War. It was young then and was wounded with gun shot, which is still buried deep inside it. It tells of the time the Indians traveled in bands and also has some arrow heads buried in it. It was a witness to the trail of tears when the Cherokee Indians were forced from their homeland and sent to Oklahoma. The old oak gave them its acorns to grind into meal and make cakes to eat. They suffered a lot and the trail they followed became known as, "The Trail of Tears."

You know Jake, that old tree has kept track of its age by adding a ring every year inside its trunk. It can also tell you if it was a good year or bad year. If it rained enough and the old leaves fertilized it, the age rings are far apart. If it was a dry year and the tree had to struggle to stay alive, the rings are close together. The tree really is a history book. If you look up in the tree you will see where the bark looks kind of scabby. That is from the settlers marking their trails with a hatchet by cutting off some of the bark until the bare wood inside showed. That is where the name of blazing a trail came from. It was a marked tree on a blazed trail through the forest.

When you visit in the winter you will find the old oak has not lost its leaves. They will be brown and rattle together when the cold north wind blows, but the leaves will not fall. The old oak made a promise to an old Indian friend years ago to keep its leaves so he would not have to leave his tribe. The tribal council had decided he had to leave when all the leaves fell off of the trees. When he had asked his old friend the oak, the oak had promised to help him. The oak remembered him as a boy who climbed its branches and was always helpful and courteous to all the members of the tribe.

"You just go ahead and climb it but remember to be very careful. I will get a ladder so you can climb up to the first branch, after that you should be able to climb it by yourself. You know some of those old limbs will let you ride them like a cowboy and they will buck you off if you are not careful. When you come back down you can tell me if you heard the voices in the tree and what the voices told you."

Jake helped Grandpa carry the ladder over to the old oak and started to climb after the ladder was secure. Grandpa watched and smiled as he saw Jake climb up the ladder to the first branch. When Jake finally conquered his climb to the first branch, he stood on it and let out a whoop. He proceeded to climb out on the branch and tried to ride it like a cowboy. He looked up and decided to climb higher. He returned to the main trunk and climbed up two more branches. He felt like he could see the whole wide world even though he wasn't even a fourth way up the tree. Grandpa heard him talking to the tree as if it was an old friend. Grandpa chuckled as he heard Jake ask the old tree.

"Do you remember when my dad and Grandpa climbed up in your branches?"

Jake was amazed when he looked up and saw the top of the tree nod yes in the wind. He then asked the old tree about its age.

Jake thought he heard the tree moan like his Grandpa does when he gets up out of his rocking chair, as the wind blew through its leaves. He knew he heard it moan an answer but he could not hear it clearly. He thought he heard it tell him it was over 200 years old. Oh well, he would ask his Grandpa how old the tree really is when he climbs back down.

Jake took the time to set and listen and let his imagination run wild like Grandpa had told him to. Jake could hear the birds singing in the tree and saw a squirrel scampering around in the top of it. He decided to climb higher. He pretended he was a mountain climber as he climbed higher. The old squirrel scolded him for invading its' territory. As Jake approached the top, the squirrel ran out to the end of a branch and jumped through the air into another tree. When Jake climbed as far as he dare, or as far as his fear would allow him, he looked out over the world. He sat on a limb and pretended to be an airplane pilot. Whenever a breeze blew through the tree, Jake would go for a ride high up in the friendly old oak.

Jake had discovered a new world in his grandpa's backyard. He was traveling into a world he would never forget and it was where his dad and Grandpa had traveled before him. The old oak was now Jake's friend and teacher. Maybe when the acorns fell in the autumn breeze he could get his grandpa to grind them and then talk Grandma into making acorn cakes like the Indians did before him. He knew from his first visit though, he would have to share them with the squirrel who also called the tree his home.

When Jake first looked down from his high lofty place, he felt a shiver of fear run through him. He was afraid at first to turn loose of the airplane branch and start his descent. It was a long way down to the ground. He yelled down to his grandpa.

"Grandpa, I don't think I can climb back down!"

Grandpa replied.

"Jake, I just heard a voice in the old oak tree. It sounded like your daddy's voice the first time he climbed the old oak. I will tell you like I told your daddy. There are two ways down out of that tree; you can fall down out of it or you can climb down. I think you will find that climbing down will be easier on your body. I know your daddy did. Oh, by the way Jake, the first time I climbed the tree to the top, I didn't think I could climb back down, but I listened to the tree like my dad told me to and the tree showed me how to get down safely."

Grandpa stood under the tree and watched as his grandson slowly came down the tree. He was hanging on for dear life to each branch. He could hear a voice in the tree that sounded just like his grandpa's voice directing him and giving him words of encouragement. When he reached the very first branch at the lower part on the tree, there stood Grandpa holding the ladder for him to safely finish his descent.

When he was safely down and sitting on the back porch step petting old Pete, he looked over at the tree and saw it beckoning with its branches for him to come back. He said.

"Grandpa, that old tree really can talk. It is motioning with its branches for me to climb it again."

Grandpa chuckled as he answered.

"Jake, it asked me and your dad to come back and explore its' lofty places as we did so many times, just as you will find that you will do this also, many many times"

POPPA, IS THERE REALLY A SANTA CLAUS?

A little blonde haired, blue eyed girl named Lauren Brooke, arrived into this world as all children arrive. Santa really should have brought her in his sleigh as she was an angel that brought joy to her poppa. As soon as she could talk, she had the words down; "No Poppa." She would sit on her great grandma's lap and look at Poppa. She would make sure Poppa was watching her as she kissed Grandma. Then she would say.

"What do you think of those apples?"

She had her special way of trying to make her Poppa think she didn't love him but when it was time for her to go home she would tell him she loved him. Poppa asked her for a hug one day and she told him.

"I gave your hug away!"

Poppa liked to try to fool this little girl. Sometimes he would act like he was washing his eyeballs but he never fooled her for a moment. When he washed both at the same time he would put them back in where they were crossed. Then he would take them back out and switch them. She would just shrug her shoulders. One day her poppa was reading the newspaper when he felt a little tap on his leg. He lowered the newspaper and saw a little blonde haired girl looking at him cross-eyed. She then closed her eyes and acted like she switched them. Then she just walked off without saying a word. She knew he had got her message loud and clear.

Every December she would help her Poppa decorate the Christmas tree. She had to examine every ornament as her great grandma un-wrapped them. Then this special little angel wanted to know about each and every one of them and her great grandma would tell her all about it. Poppa couldn't tell her about them but Granny could. She not only remembered when she got each one but who gave it to her or where she bought it. Little Lauren would let Poppa hold her up so she could put the angel on top of the tree.

As the years came and went, she became very proficient at decorating the tree. It was a job just for her and Poppa to do together. One year Zack, her little brother and Austin her cousin tried to help her put the ornaments on the tree. This disgusted her. They were invading in on her territory and she was not happy about it. Every decoration they put on the tree she would take back off and re-hang when they weren't looking. She didn't even want them to sing Christmas carols with her poppa.

Poppa keeps a little Christmas tree with a star on top in his den year around. Lauren decided one Halloween she wanted to be a golden girl with a magic wand. The magic wand had to have a gold star on it so now Poppa's little Christmas tree has a little angel sitting proudly on top. She never returned the gold star or let Poppa play with her magic wand so he went to his wood shop and made him self one. He even put a little music box on his magic wand that plays, "Twinkle Twinkle Little Star." She fell in love with it but Poppa wouldn't let her play with it until he could play with her magic wand. She played with it anyway. Somehow Poppa still has the little magic wand he made but expects it to disappear at any time since it is magic.

This same little blonde haired girl became known as, "Margaret," to her poppa. It was from a song they both liked to hear. Poppa won't tell you the name of the song but he would tell her when he saw her, "It is me again Margaret." He is the only one who can call her that. He threatened to call her Margaret at her high school graduation but he decided not to in front of her friends to her relief.

Now little Margaret did let her guard down one time and showed her Poppa what she did think of him. When he was in the hospital recovering from heart surgery, the telephone rang. Granny answered the phone and found little Lauren on the other end of the line. She asked to speak to Poppa. When Poppa put the receiver to his ear he heard the best medicine he could ever receive. A little voice said.

"I love you Poppa."

This little blue eyed angel was always having poems written about her by Poppa. She represented Christmas to him and always helped decorate the tree so he found this poem sitting at the tips of his fingers one December when she was but a little blonde haired angel.

CHRISTMAS GIRL

The Christmas tree lights were burning,
When a knock came upon the door.
When the door was opened,
Little feet skipped across the floor.

Into the den those little feet go,
As upon the carpet they dance.
To check to see if Santa,
Had left a gift by any chance.

A little girl's blue eyes sparkled,
When indeed she found a gift.
But it was her old Poppa,
Who really received a lift.

Christmas is present whenever,
This little angel is around.
She took time to play the little organ,
As she made a happy sound.

She received a Christmas gift,
But her Poppa did too you'll see.
His special Christmas present,
Was dancing by the Christmas tree.

Time must pass and when Lauren was six or seven years old, she was helping her Poppa decorate the tree. All of a sudden she turned to Poppa and said.

"Poppa, is there really a Santa Claus?"

Poppa looked at her and asked.

"Why do you ask such a question?"

Lauren faced him squarely and replied.

"Because some of my friends at school say there is not a Santa Claus."

Poppa cleared his throat and replied.

"Lauren, I believe in Christmas. It is a time when a little baby was born unto this world in a stable. It is a time to give, share and love. I have Christmas in my heart and always will. If you believe in Christmas and have it in your heart, then there is a Santa Claus."

Lauren never asked Poppa again if there was a Santa Claus and continued helping him decorate the Christmas tree until the time came when she moved away. Poppa to this day still watches and listens for Santa on Christmas Eve.

THE OLD COWBOY AND SANTA

SANTA was flying along on his midnight ride delivering Christmas presents to families living in central Wyoming. He was keeping a sharp eye out to make sure he did not miss anyone this Christmas Eve. The ranches were far apart over this sparse countryside. He spotted a little campfire and decided he had better stop and check. He slowed his reindeer and approached the campfire with the moon at his back. He settled down with a gentle landing and came to a halt close to the fire. He was surprised to see a lone old cowboy sitting by the campfire with a skinny old horse tethered close by. He wore a beat up old hat and his clothes were well worn. Santa gave his usual HO, HO, HO, and a Merry Christmas. The old cowboy eyed him a moment and then through a toothless grin said.

"Git on out of that rig and come on over for a bite to eat. I got a pan of beans cooking here on the fire. As red as your face is I'd say you need to set by the campfire and git yourself warm."

Santa hopped out of his sleigh and walked over to the old cowboy and introduced himself. The old cowboy shook Santa's hand as he said.

"Howdy Santa, you can just call me, Wyoming, everybody else

does."

Santa immediately took a liking to Wyoming. Wyoming dished Santa up a hot plate of beans and gave him a piece of hardtack. As they ate, Santa eyed the old cowboy and said.

"You have been so kind to share your meal with me. I am delivering presents this Christmas Eve; is there anything you would like to have for a present this Christmas?"

Wyoming scratched his chin as he thought for a moment. He had heard of Santa and remembered how his mother and dad had celebrated Christmas when he was small. His parents were gone now and he was alone grubbing a living with his old horse, Paint, herding a few scrawny cattle. It was lonely out here in the middle of nowhere. He glanced over at the reindeer team patiently waiting for Santa. They looked liked they would be good eating. He wondered how Santa had caught them and trained them to pull the sleigh that flew. He figured Santa would not part with any his reindeer. He thought back again to his youth and the one box of crayons his mother had given him. He had never gone to school, his mother had taught him how to read and write and that was all. When she had given him the box of crayons she had cautioned him about breaking them. She had told him there would be no more ever, so take care of them. The very first day he had broken the red crayon. He tried and tried to fix it but to no avail. He never did get another box of crayons and he had used everyone until there was nothing left. Wyoming looked at Santa and said.

"Santa, in my life time I have only had one box of crayons. I would like to have a box of crayons and sketch paper." I have always wanted to draw what I see out here in this pretty country."

Santa was surprised at Wyoming request but never questioned him. He walked over to the sleigh and soon returned with a new box of crayons, a sketch pad, and a sack of dry beans. He handed them to the old cowboy as he said.

"Merry Christmas Wyoming, and thank you for sharing your meal with me. I must be on my way to finish my deliveries. I will be looking for your campfire next year."

Wyoming thanked Santa for the Christmas presents. He watched as Santa jumped into his sleigh and disappeared among the stars in the vast night sky. Not only did Wyoming watch Santa leave, but Paint his old friend and work partner was watching also. As Paint watched, he wished he could fly, this rocky country made his feet sore. The next day as they were out looking for strays, Paint tried leaping in the air to fly but to no avail. Wyoming thought his old horse was just trying to be frisky.

Santa did keep his promise and every year he would scan the countryside for the old cowboy's lonely campfire. When he would see it, he would land and as always, Wyoming had a pot of beans to share. Wyoming would show Santa all the pictures he had sketched of the countryside during the last year. One year he gave Santa a sketch of him sitting by the campfire with his sleigh and reindeer in the background. Santa was very proud of it and had Mrs. Claus frame it and hang it over the fire place. Santa kept Wyoming supplied with sketch pads and crayons every Christmas Eve. He also kept his old friend supplied with dry beans. In addition to crayons he introduces Wyoming to colored pencils to sketch with. Santa found out Wyoming was a great artist and could put on paper what he saw through his eyes.

One year Santa searched and searched the vast snow covered landscape below for his old friend. He was about to give up when he spotted a small flicker from a campfire. When he landed he found Wyoming laying next to the fire and just barely breathing. Paint was standing over his old friend on shaky legs. Both of them did not have much longer to be on the range. Santa stood for a moment and looked into the few embers flickering in the campfire. He knew the embers of life were leaving his friend and his faithful horse.

Santa went back to his sleigh and returned with a small can of powder he kept just for special occasions such as this. He sprinkled a very small amount of it on Wyoming and Paint as he said.

"Wyoming my old friend, I need you to be one of my helpers as an elf at the North Pole. You will work in Toyland overseeing all the western children clothing and cowboy toys. All the rocking horses will be under your supervision. You will also see there are enough crayons in the Toyland inventory so each and every child can have a box of crayons. Paint you have been a faithful friend to Wyoming and I know he would want you to be at the North Pole with him. You will be one of my reindeer for tonight and help pull the sleigh. When we get to the North Pole I have a special stall with plenty of feed for you to retire in. Wyoming can come down to the reindeer barn and feed and visit with you every day."

Santa watched as Wyoming stirred and slowly changed into an elf still dressed in his old cowboy clothes, beat up hat, and boots with run over heels. Then Santa and his cowboy elf friend harnessed Paint the reindeer, and hitched him to the sleigh. Santa walked over to what remained of the campfire and kicked snow on it and made sure all the embers of life were out. Wyoming sat next to Santa as they departed this cold barren countryside and climbed up in the moon lit sky. Wyoming was impressed with the view below. He must sketch it when he gets to his new home. Paint was now flying, carrying his old friend to the north range and an easier life ahead.

LITTLE TOOT'S FINAL CHRISTMAS TRIP

GRAMPS was sitting in his recliner listening to Christmas carols as he watched Little Toot resting on the tiny tracks under the Christmas tree. Little Toot appeared to have something bothering him and was restless. The last few years Little Toot had carried kindergarten students to visit Santa at the North Pole. Gramps and Little Toot had been friends for years and Gramps could tell his little friend was dreaming.

Santa had again sent Wayne the Christmas tree elf to visit Gramps and Little Toot. He was sitting up in the Christmas tree eating candy canes and watching Little Toot sleep. He took a small branch and bent it down and tickled Little Toot on his smoke stack. Toot blinked his tiny head light and let a tiny puff of smoke rise from his smoke stack. Wayne chuckled and tickled him again. Toot sighed and released a little steam. Wayne climbed down out of the tree and walked over to Gramps. He handed him a note from Santa inviting two kindergarten classes Gramps visits to come to Toyland to be Santa's guests. The note went on to say how lonely Mrs. Claus was and how she would love company. Wayne walked back over to Little Toot and put a sack of magic flying powder in the engine cab. He turned and winked at Gramps and disappeared as fast as he had appeared. His job was done for Santa and now it was up to Little Toot and Gramps to make arrangements with the elementary principal and kindergarten teachers.

The very next day Gramps went to school and talked to the elementary principal, Mrs. Middleton, to discuss the invitation Wayne, the Christmas tree elf had delivered. She wanted to go also and agreed to let the classes go with their parent's approval. Gramps then visited the kindergarten classrooms and talked to Mrs. Debbie Finch and Mrs. Elaine Williams and told them of the invitation Santa had given. They both agreed they thought their classes would love to go on the trip. They sent notes home with their students the very next day informing the parents about the trip and asked for their parent's approval to visit Santa at the North Pole.

It was decided the following individuals would accompany the classes on Little Toot to the North Pole.

Mrs. Angie Middleton-Elementary Principal

Mrs. Tiffany Kennemore-Elementary Assistant Principal

Mrs. Shelia King-Elementary Secretary

Mrs. Amber Stewart-Elementary Secretary

Gramps-Train Engineer

Ken Finch-Assistant engineer and navigator

KINDERGARTEN CLASSES

Mrs. Debbie Finch-Teacher	Mrs. Elaine Williams-Teacher
Corey	Austin
Alexander (Alex)	Ethan
Kayla	Shalee

Alexandra	Ziara
Payton	Bryan
Abiud	Cole
Jacob	Justin
Kameron	Haley
Keighlyn	Jesse
Ty	Hailie
Korey	Germany
Antonicia	Blake
Sarah	Silas
James	Jordan
Elizabeth	Caleb
Selena	Elizabeth
Fabian	Mason
Sara	Cameron
Madison	Shakiya
Luke	

Wayne the Christmas tree elf returned to the North Pole and reported to Santa that his message had been delivered. Santa turned on his wall screen in his office to monitor Gramps and Little Toot. He watched and listened as Gramps talked to the principal and kindergarten teachers. He was pleased to hear they were all in favor of accepting his invitation. He watched as the teachers gave each student a note to take home to get their parent's permission to go on the trip. He didn't have to wait long as within three days all notes had been returned to the teachers and every parent gave their permission. As soon as Santa found out his invitation had been accepted, he informed Mrs. Claus. She was beside herself and started immediately making arrangements with the elf ladies.

The children were all excited about the upcoming trip to the North Pole to visit Santa. Each class had helped their teacher decorate the Christmas tree in the classroom. The teachers had made a list of what each of their students would like to see at the North Pole or ask Santa. The teachers would give the list to Santa when they arrived to visit him. The list is as follows for Mrs. Finch's class.

Selena - I want to ask Santa for a Nintendo D.S., a baby doll, and a real cat.

Korey - I want to ask Santa bring me an 18 wheeler.

Antonicia - I want to ask Santa for a Hannah Montana doll and two books.

Sara - I want to ask Santa for a Hannah Montana Christmas doll.

Keighlyn - I want to ask Santa to see his reindeer and an elf. I want "Bolt" the dog movie and a nintendo D.S.

Madison - I want to ask Santa to bring me a game and a movie.

Luke - I want to ask Santa for a toy.

Alex - I want to ask Santa to bring me a toy airplane.

Payton - I want to ask Santa to bring me a tractor and a D.S.

Ty - I want to see frozen water at the North Pole.

Sarah - I want to see a bird at the North Pole.

Trey - I just want to see Santa.

Corey - I want to see Rudolph, an elf, and Santa.

Abiud - I want to see snow at the North Pole.

Kameron - I want to see toys.

Kayla - I want to see Santa's reindeer.

Alexandra - I want to ask Santa to bring me a Barbie in the diamond castle with 2 Barbies and 2 puppies.

Fabien - I want to see snow at the North Pole.

Elizabeth - I want to ask Santa for a Barbie house and a Barbie.

Jake - I want to ask Santa to bring me a "Bolt" movie.

The following is a list of Mrs. William's class.

Hailie - I would like to meet his elves.

Haley - I would like to see Santa Claus.

Bryan - I would like to ask Santa for a Spiderman toy.

Jesse - I would like to be an elf.

Austin - I would like to ask Santa for a bike.

Ethan - I want to be an elf and make a motorcycle to do a wheelie.

Germany - I would ask for a toy please.

Jordan - I would tell Santa I love him and ask him for an art desk.

Shalee - I would ask him for a Barbie house.

Blake - I would ask him for a motorcycle that goes a million mile an hour and a million dollars.

Mason - I would ask to be Santa's helper.

Cameron - I would ask Santa for a dirt bike.

Caleb - I would ask for a race car.

Elizabeth - I would ask him for a Barbie house with Barbies.

Ziara - I would ask for a girl motorcycle.

Cole - I want a dirt bike that's real and super fast and my size.

Silas - I'd ask him for a wrestling game.

Shakiya - I would ask him for a dog.

Justin - I'd ask Santa for a bike.

They had a hard time keeping their minds on their studies and then there was the Christmas play they would perform for their parents. Mrs. Finch's class would perform the play, "Miracles in The Old Barn." It is about school children getting stranded during a snow storm and taking refuge in an old barn where the animals take care of them. The children had been practicing everyday and were excited but nervous. Gramps even gets to narrate the play.

Mrs. William's class will sing Christmas carols for their Christmas program for the parents. They practiced hard every school day and had finally learned the words to all the carols they were going to sing. They even practiced at home so their parents already knew what the program would consist of. The closer the day came though for them to sing, the larger the stage became. Gramps would get to be on the stage with this class also and read them a story about, "The Best Christmas Ever." The children knew though the trip to the North Pole would be the best Christmas ever. They had decorated and undecorated the Christmas tree in their classroom a hundred times. Under the tree was their list to Santa, which would be hand delivered to him.

The trip to the North Pole would start the day after Christmas vacation begins and they would stay two full days sight seeing and visiting Santa and Mrs. Claus. Gramps planned to use the runway at the airport across the highway from the school. This would give Little Toot plenty of runaway to see if he could really fly. He had flown the year before with the magic flying powder Santa had furnished to mix with his coal. Gramps had double checked Little Toot's cab to make sure the magic flying powder Wayne the Christmas tree elf had left would be enough to fly the round trip to the North Pole.

Time passed so slow for the anxious students. They wanted the day to come when they would start their trip to visit Santa, but they were also apprehensive when it came to getting on that big stage in front of everyone to perform their Christmas program. The day finally did come and Mrs. Finch's class was so excited they forgot their fears as they sang and acted out their part performing the animals and the snow bound school students in the old barn. Mrs. William's class took the stage when it was their turn and sang their practiced Christmas carols to perfection. When each class finished their program, they received a standing ovation. A few tears had been shed by some of the children at first but they soon wiped them away when they discovered they were actually enjoying themselves and that no one would hurt them. Gramps said he was afraid someone may come up on the stage and get him but no one did. Mrs. Finch had told him not to worry because she didn't know anyone who would waste their time coming up on the stage to get him.

After the programs were finished, Gramps spent the rest of the day getting Little Toot ready for his flight. The Pullman cars were cleaned and ready for the children. The dining car had fresh table cloths and all the cooking and serving utensils were clean and ready for use. The baggage car was empty and ready to store the extra luggage required for the trip. The Arctic gear would have to be loaded into the Pullman car and the passengers would need to wear it before the trip was over.

The next morning Granny put the homemade cookies she had baked in the dining car for the children to munch on during their trip.

Gramps ate a hearty breakfast and then threw his gear in Little Toot's cab. He fired up the boiler on Little Toot's engine and while it was building steam he hugged Granny good-by and then climbed up in the cab. When the steam pressure was high enough, Gramps cracked open the throttle and Little Toot slowly pulled out of the driveway and within a few minutes was pulling onto the school grounds where the children were waiting with their parents. Gramps brought Little Toot to a full stop in front of the elementary office.

The parents stood back and watched as their children started boarding the train. The teachers called the roll and the children boarded as their name was called. After the children were on the train and were all accounted for, the baggage was loaded in the baggage car along with the decorated classroom Christmas trees. The children wanted to take their decorated classroom Christmas trees to Santa and the elves. Gramps had informed them that it is too cold to grow trees at the North Pole. The arctic clothing and bunny boots were loaded in the Pullman cars. Mrs. Middleton had been checking and double checking as everybody boarded and all the needed supplies were loaded and stored. Ken had gone to operations and filed the flight plan. He had just returned when Mrs. Middleton signaled Gramps that they were ready to depart. Gramps and Ken climbed up in the cab of Little Toot. Gramps cracked the throttle on Little Toot and as the train slowly pulled out the children pressed their noses against the windows as they waved to their parents.

The flight plan Ken had filed was direct to Branson, Missouri. Gramps had been to Branson, Missouri recently and attended the show, "A tribute to John Denver." While at this show Granny and he had found out about a Foster Ranch for abused and neglected children. The ranch is named, "Jacob's House at Thunder Ranch," located just outside of Branson. Some children wait forever to be placed in a foster home but not at Thunder Ranch. The wait is over for these children. The doors are open to them at Jacob's House at Thunder Ranch.

Jacob's House at Thunder Ranch located just outside Branson, Missouri, is on seventy acres. Thunder Ranch is comprised of individual homes. Christian adults are licensed by the Division of Family Services and are provided a beautiful home to provide direction, encouragement, accountability, and loving discipline for traumatized, neglected and abused children. In exchange, each foster parent is dedicated to raising someone else's children through sacrificial Christian service.

When Granny and Gramps learned about this program they decided to support it. Gramps thought it would be educational for the kindergarten classes to tour Thunder Ranch and then take the students for a ride in the amphibious Duck Rides through the Festival of Lights in Branson. After the tour of lights it would be time for a good nights rest in the Pullman cars. After a good nights sleep, it would be time for Little Toot to be landing at the North Pole. Gramps had given Mrs. Middleton the plan for her approval, which she readily did.

With the flight plan filed and all were aboard on Little Toot, Gramps proceeded to the runway on the Aeroplex. When they arrived at the end of the runway, Gramps notified the control tower and requested permission to proceed onto the active runway. The tower gave them clearance to proceed to runway three-zero. Gramps double checked the magic flying powder from Santa was mixed with the fuel. After Little Toot was lined upon the active runway, the tower gave them permission to takeoff. Gramps opened the throttle and reported to the tower they were rolling. When the throttle was opened for takeoff, little fins extended from the side of the engine and each car like tiny wings. Gramps watched in amazement but figured this was from the magic flying powder. They even had tiny ailerons and flaps on these wings. Little Toot gained speed and when he lifted off the runway the tower was informed. Gramps set up climb power until they reached fifteen hundred feet then set cruise power. From this altitude the students will be able to see the landscape during the flight to Branson. Ken gave Little Toot the heading toward Branson, Missouri. The trip to the North Pole via Branson had begun.

During the trip to Branson the two classes enjoyed the scenery and were amazed at the amount of woodland in the state of Arkansas. They could see the flat lands broken by a ridge known as Crowley Ridge. Then the lay of the land was flat again for a few miles. They could see the Ozarks rising up in front of them as they continued their trip west by northwest. They saw Norfolk Lake and the Lake of the Ozarks. Several of the students had been there on vacation to fish and campout. Some had even tried to water ski and taken hard falls, but their parents had told them that was part of learning.

When Branson was in sight, they started a slow let down and landed as softly as a feather. Transportation was waiting to take them to Thunder Ranch. They were taken on a tour of the whole ranch and got to visit with the children. Not only did the children get to visit the ranch but unknown to the children, Santa and Rufus were watching on the big North Pole screen. Santa was pleased the students were taking the time to visit these children. He noted in his special book to deliver each and every one of these foster children a special gift. The kindergarten classes were also all treated to a hot meal along with all the adults escorting them. The time passed too quickly and soon dusk was settling over the land. They boarded back onto their transportation and were each given a Santa stocking cap to keep their heads warm when they rode on the ducks. Soon they were on their way to Branson for the ride on the ducks to tour the Festival of Lights.

They were all eyes as they traveled through Branson and looked at all the Christmas decoration on their way to the Festival of Lights. The whole town was one big Christmas tree. Gramps enjoyed it as much as the children. The tour of the Festival of Lights was a festival. It left not a thing to the imagination. Lighted reindeer pulling a sleigh was enjoyed by all. They had a Nativity Scene and stars lighting the way. The students enjoyed the tour and it was over too soon even though they were exhausted from a busy long day.

They returned to where Little Toot had been patiently waiting.

Little Toot had kept the little train warm and well lit. After they were back on the train, they were served hot cocoa and cookies. Then it was time for the children to be escorted to the Pullman cars and tucked in bed. Not one of them objected. Meanwhile Gramps had returned to the engine while Ken filed the flight plan for a direct flight to the North Pole. The estimated time of arrival was 0700 hours the next morning. When Ken returned to the cab of Little Toot, Mrs. Middleton informed Ken and Gramps that all were aboard and ready for departure. Ken showed a desire to handle the controls on takeoff and Gramps readily agreed. He wanted to watch the Christmas lights as they climbed out to cruising altitude.

Little Toot took to the air with Ken at the controls and Gramps scooping some coal with the magic flying powder mixed in it. Amber and Shelia had snuck back to the caboose to view the lights during the takeoff and climb to cruise altitude. Mrs. Finch and Mrs. Williams were in the Pullman cars with their students. Mrs. Middleton and Mrs. Kennemore were in the dining car enjoying a hot cup of cocoa and Granny's home made cookies. Gramps and Ken took turns at the controls as they journeyed to the North Pole. They were entertained by the Christmas lights in the cities below as they passed overhead. The northern lights appeared brightly in the sky as they flew northward. They were swirling and dancing in the sky ahead.

Around six A.M. Gramps and Ken saw two figures dressed in Arctic gear crawling over the coal car behind the engine. As they watched they were amazed to see it was Amber and Shelia. They had decided just once they wanted to ride in the cab of Little Toot and view the Northern Lights. They also wanted to see what it was like landing up front in the cab. Gramps and Ken welcomed the company and even offered to share the coal scoop shovel with them. When the North Pole and Toyland were in sight, Little Toot joyfully blew his whistle. Gramps eased back on the throttle and lined up on the North Pole runway to land.

Santa was just coming out of the reindeer barn when he heard Little Toot's whistle. He had just finished watering and feeding his reindeer. He told Rufus to have the helper elves open the door to the special shed for Little Toot. This would keep the children warm when they got off of the train. Little Toot needed a special shed also to keep from freezing since the temperature was frigid. Santa glanced up at his house and saw Mrs. Claus wiping her hands on her apron and scanning the sky for her visitors. He knew she had been listening for Little Toot's whistle every since she had woke up that morning. Mrs. Claus and some elf lady friends had been busy fixing a big breakfast for the expected visitors. They knew their visitors would be hungry and would need the energy for a busy scheduled day.

Santa watched as Little Toot made a perfect landing on the North Pole runway. He saw the little wings retract on the engine and cars after Little Toot had came to a full stop. The elves had a follow me sleigh at the end of the runway to greet Little Toot and show him where to park for his stay. When Little Toot pulled into the special shed next to Toyland, Mrs. Claus and Santa along with the Elf families were waiting there to greet their visitors. After Little Toot had come to a full stop, Santa and Mrs. Claus gave each and every passenger a big hug as they got off of the train. Of course Santa had to welcome the children with his merry, Ho, Ho, Ho. Mrs. Middleton introduced Mrs. Elaine Williams and Mr. Ken Finch to the Claus and the Elf families. All the other adults had been to the North Pole before and had met the Clauses and the Elf families. After the big welcome was complete, Mrs. Claus informed Mrs. Middleton that a hot breakfast was waiting to be served to everyone. Santa and Gramps heard her loud and clear and made sure there would be no lollygagging.

As they were walking to Mr. and Mrs. Claus's home for breakfast, Mrs. Finch has some news she just had to share. She held onto Santa's arm and led him over by Mrs. Claus. As they all walked arm in arm she said.

"Mr. Finch and I are Grandparents to a little girl named, Kambree. She is the joy of our life and we can't wait to celebrate her first Christmas."

Mrs. Claus stopped and hugged Mr. and Mrs. Finch and congratulated them. Santa also gave his congratulations and then he winked at Gramps as he said.

"Mrs. Finch, you aren't fluffy enough to be a grandma. Grandmas are supposed to be fluffy so their grandchildren will have a soft place to sit and lay on."

Mrs. Claus gave her husband a gentle tap and told him to "shush." Santa just grinned and then started walking faster when he thought about the hot biscuits and gravy waiting to be eaten.

After they had washed their hands and faces, they sat down at the breakfast table. Santa asked that everyone join hands while he said Grace. After he had blessed the meal and said thanks for the safe arrival of his guests, it was time to eat. Mrs. Shelia King and Mrs. Amber Stewart sat next to Santa. They had decided during the trip to the North Pole that they were going to sit next to him at least once during a meal. They had always been amazed at the amount of food he consumed and his like for biscuits and gravy. He always left some on his whiskers and would take his napkin and wipe his beard around his mouth when he was finished. They also had noticed that he was always jolly and smelled refreshing. They loved his sense of humor and decided he smelled like peppermint. Even after being in the barn with his reindeer he smelled like peppermint they remembered. As they sat next to him they discovered why, he had peppermint sticks in his pockets to nibble on as he went about his work.

They finally let their curiosity get the best of them and asked him about the peppermint sticks. Santa put his fork loaded with biscuits and gravy down and with a twinkle in his eye said.

"I used to smoke a pipe all the time. People were complaining I stunk their house up when I delivered presents on Christmas Eve. Mrs. Claus even complained about me smoking in her house and stinking it up. I couldn't smoke in the reindeer barn because my pipe may set the barn on fire; so one day I just decided to give it up. Smoking pipe tobacco is habit forming so I started nibbling on peppermint sticks to help break the habit. Now you know why I smell like peppermint and Mrs. Claus is so happy. She rewards me with biscuits and gravy every morning."

Santa picked up his fork and made his biscuits and gravy disappear under Shelia and Amber's watchful eyes. Everyone ate a hearty meal and after they were through eating, Gramps asked if there were any volunteers to help him unload the decorated Christmas trees. The kindergarten classes decided they wanted to get the tree from their own classroom and give to Santa. They decided one should be placed in Santa's home and the other in Toyland for all to enjoy. It seems that Gramps had pilfered the decorated Christmas tree Mrs. Finch's class had used for their play and secretly loaded it on the train. He wanted it placed in the barn. It had been used in the play, Miracles in the Old Barn, so he felt it should be put in Santa's barn, since Santa was the one responsible for the miracle.

While the Christmas trees were being unloaded and set up under the watchful eye of Wayne the Christmas tree elf, the other elf men unloaded the baggage and delivered it to the appropriate homes. Santa's dog Clarence had a keen interest in the trees and was happy to see one of the trees put in the barn where he stayed.

Mrs. Finch and Mrs. Williams classes helped set up the decorated Christmas tree in Toyland as Santa watched. When the tree was in place, the teachers gave Santa the list which showed what the students wanted to see at the North Pole or wanted to ask Santa. Santa already knew what was on the list. He had eavesdropped on them as the classes had told their teachers their answers.

Santa was especially happy to see on the list where a student had followed his request with the magic word "please." The children who had asked to see snow on ice or meet the elves or Santa would also receive other presents on Christmas Eve. As Santa read the list, he took the time to talk to each student and give each one a hug. He thanked the teachers for taking the time to make the list for their students and for the Christmas trees. He then gave each of the teachers a hug. He examined the Christmas tree they had brought to Toyland. It had the special touch children give a tree when they help decorate them. He also noticed Wayne the Christmas tree elf had added his special touch by making the branches lighter by removing goodies, which had hung on it.

Afterwards Santa took the classes on a tour of Toyland. As they were touring he asked each one if they would like to help the elves fill the Christmas orders for other children around the world. If they wanted to help, they were given a choice where they wanted to work. Several of the girls wanted to help in the doll section. The boys were more interested in motorcycles and four wheelers. Boys and girls alike showed their interest in the electronic games, of which there was an endless amount of different games. Santa saw on the list where some of the children wanted to see his reindeer. He promised to show the children his reindeer and take them on a sleigh ride through the Northern Lights before their visit was over.

When the tour was over, Santa asked his elf workers in Toyland to care for the classes and let them work where ever they chose. He told Mrs. Finch and Mrs. Williams to go back to the house and visit with Mrs. Claus and the other ladies. He planned to go to the barn and check on his reindeer and visit with Ken and Gramps. He knew Gramps but he wanted to find out more about Mr. Finch and get on a first name basis with him. He also was interested in finding out all the news since he had visited with Gramps last.

Santa returned to the barn and found Ken and Gramps sitting on a bale of hay taking a snooze. When he came in the barn and saw them relaxing he just had to yell, Ho, Ho, Ho, and woke them up. Gramps and Ken woke up looking into the smiling face of Santa. Santa pulled up another bale of hay and sat down to get acquainted with Ken and shoot the buck. In other words, they were going to exchange stories rather they were true or not. It wasn't long until their laughter could be heard all the way to the house where the ladies were visiting.

The elves were letting the children work and play in Toyland. They even pitched in to help wrap presents. They would hand the tape and bows to the elves as they wrapped presents. As the students worked and played in Toyland, they saw an old toothless elf working with three other elves making rocking horses and western clothing. They were also packing up little cowboy outfits for the little partners anxiously waiting for Santa. They asked Rufus, the head elf, about this cowboy elf. Rufus told them this elf's name is Wyoming and is a special friend of Santa. Rufus escorted all the students over to meet Wyoming. Wyoming greeted all of them with his toothless grin and a "Howdy." Wyoming was also in charge of school and art supplies. He gave each student a box of crayons and told them to be careful and not break them as each one was special. He promised to show them his reindeer horse when they toured the barn the next day. Three of the students who liked horses and western toys volunteered to help the old cowboy. He was pleased to have the help and the company. He had not been around children much in his lifetime but they sure seemed a joy to him.

The rest of the students with Rufus just had to find out if Rufus or Gramps was older. Rufus grinned as he informed them he knew Gramps when he wore knickers. The children wanted to know what knickers are but all Rufus would tell them was, go ask Gramps if he ever wore knickers. Rufus knew Gramps would smile and not tell them the truth. He also knew the children would keep questioning him until they got an answer.

The morning passed quickly and it was time for lunch. The children ate lunch with the Elf families they were staying with. The children were surprised when they found out they would be eating pizza. They all loved pizza but never dreamed they would be eating it at the North Pole. Gramps and the other adult visitors had dinner with the Claus's. They had mashed potatoes with brown gravy and all the trimmings. For dessert they made a hot peach cobbler disappear except what was left on Santa's beard.

After dinner, all pitched in to clear the table and wash the dishes except Santa and Gramps, who quick-stepped it and were soon out of sight. Ken soon joined them in the barn where they had some serious matters to study as they rested their eyes. The kindergarten teachers along with Amber and Shelia spent part of the afternoon with the students in Toyland. They found the new items Santa's elves had created were fascinating. Grandma Finch saw so many gifts she just had to get for her granddaughter. There were baby dolls that did everything except housework. These ladies are all mothers and saw items they knew their own children would love to receive for Christmas. Mrs. Finch did lay claim on a special rocking horse Wyoming had handcrafted. She could use it in her Christmas play when Kambree was not occupying it.

In the middle of the afternoon, Santa along with his two sidekicks showed up at Toyland. They gave all the children rides on snowmobiles. Then they took them ice skating on a special indoor ice pond Santa had made for the elf children. Santa chuckled as he watched the children try to skate for their first time. They spent more time falling down and getting up than they did skating. Santa put on a pair of old skates and surprised everyone watching as he glided gracefully around the pond and even did a few jumps. He then held on to the children's hands and gave them ice skating lessons. He even got Shelia and Amber to ice skate with him. Finally, he talked Mrs. Williams into skating with him but try as he may, he could not get Mrs. Finch out on the ice. Mrs. Williams surprised Santa with how well she could skate. When they finished skating they all went into Toyland and enjoyed hot chocolate and cookies. They all had red noses and rosy cheeks.

The time pasted too quickly for the children as they worked in Toyland. Try as they may, they never saw all the things being manufactured for presents. To their surprise, when they left Toyland they were escorted back to the indoor ice skating pond where several bonfires were burning under the old cowboy elf's watchful eye. The lady elves had put blankets for the children to sit on as they roasted hot dogs and marshmallows. They were joined by Mrs. Claus and Santa along with all the adult chaperons and the elf families. Even Santa's old hound Clarence, joined them. When the children roasted their hotdogs and marshmallows, they also had to roast extra for Clarence. As they sat by the fires, everyone joined in singing Christmas carols. It was a time the kindergarten students would never forget.

As the old cowboy elf watched and listened, he thought back to the times he had sat alone by his campfire listening to it crackle. The only other sounds he would hear were of his cattle bedded down nearby and his horse digging through the snow for dry grass. The wolves would be talking to each other in the distance as they searched the cold night for a morsel to eat. The old cowboy smiled as he listened to the children sing. He was so pleased Santa was a special friend and had given him his new home. Wyoming reached into his pocket and pulled out his old harmonica. To Santa's surprise, the old cowboy started playing the Christmas carols the children were singing.

Now the fire started to turn to embers and all the children were well fed, it was time for them to turn in for a good night's sleep. It had been a full day for everyone. After the children were all tucked in, Santa, Gramps, Ken and Wyoming sat around a small fire just like the old cowboy use to sit by. The old cowboy had built the small campfire earlier and put on a large pot of beans to cook. They were watching that big pot of beans cook and enjoying the aroma it made. When the beans were done, the ladies joined them around the fire for a bowl of beans, hardtack and a friendly visit. Santa smiled at Wyoming as they all ate. Mrs. Claus was beside herself with all this friendly company. When it was time for all of them to call it a day, Mrs. Claus surprised everyone when she walked over to the old cowboy elf, and as she gave him a hug she whispered.

"Wyoming, I want to thank you for such a very special time. Santa and I wish you a Merry Christmas."

Before the old cowboy turned in for the night, he walked to the barn to talk to his faithful old reindeer horse. He had to wipe a tear from his eye. He had never had a lady hug him since his own mother had hugged him. Yes, this is a Merry Christmas. He heard a rustling over by the Christmas tree in the barn. He saw Clarence the hound and Wayne the Christmas tree elf watching him. After he gave old Paint an extra bit of grain, he walked over and set by the Christmas tree with them. They all sat in silence as they listened to the sounds of the night. It had been a very special day.

The children were up bright and early the next day. Santa had promised to take them for a sleigh ride through the swirling northern lights. The children ate breakfast with the elf families they were staying with. They found all the furnishing in the elf houses were just the right size for them to fit in comfortably. The lady elves let the children watch and help as they prepared breakfast. They fixed hot cereal which most of the students turned their noses up at. They were more interested in pancakes with hot butter and a fruit topping along with whip cream. The children did not realize the whip cream was from reindeer. They enjoyed the donuts and cinnamon rolls the ladies took the time to make. They were also offered different kinds of dry cereal and milk.

While the children were eating their breakfast, Santa had said Grace and was enjoying a hearty breakfast with his company. He had a half dozen fresh biscuits and gravy stacked on his dish and was devouring them under the watchful eye of Mrs. Kennemore. She had decided it was her turn to sit by Santa at the breakfast table. Of course Santa did not object. She did notice the gravy that was collecting on his beard. She knew from experience he would take care of the extra gravy when he was finished eating his fill. Gramps was enjoying his pancakes and eggs.

After breakfast, Mrs. Finch and Mrs. Williams helped clear the table and then went to check on their students. Santa with his two sidekicks headed to the barn to feed the reindeer. After the reindeer were fed, Santa and Rufus started putting the harness on the reindeer team. Santa asked Gramps and Ken if they would check to see when the children would be ready for their sleigh ride. Gramps and Ken soon reappeared in the barn door with all the children following closely behind. They were all bubbling over with excitement. Santa and Rufus hitched the reindeer team to the sleigh as the children watched from the barn door. Clarence made his rounds among the children getting a pet from each one.

By the time the reindeers and sleigh were ready, the ladies had finished the dishes and were ready to join the children on the sleigh ride. While one sleigh load was touring the northern lights display, the others were up in the hayloft swinging on a hay rope and acting like trapeze artist. Old cowboy appeared and put a saddle on his reindeer horse, Paint. He had promised the children a ride on old Paint and he and Paint both were looking forward to the exercise. Santa was having the time of his life entertaining the children and their chaperons. He let those who wanted to, hold the reins and drive the reindeer as they sailed through the swirling lights and they all got their turn.

Gramps and Ken helped watch the children to see that none got too rambunctious and got hurt. The children could be heard for miles as they played in the hayloft and squealed with delight. After all had their turn riding through the swirling aurora borealis, the reindeer team was unhitched and put back in their stalls where they received a good ration of feed and a good brushing. Paint was enjoying carrying the children on his back as his old friend Wyoming led him around the reindeer barnyard.

The morning passed quickly and it was time for lunch. Everyone gathered at the North Pole Community center for sandwiches and French fries. They had a choice of barbecue, hot dogs, or hamburger sandwiches. Santa tried them all along with Gramps. For dessert their choices ranged from cookies, cake, or several different kinds of pie. Again, Santa tried them all to the enjoyment and amazement of the children. After the lunch had been served, the children returned to the elf homes for a much needed rest. The men headed for the barn to see if a certain bale of hay needed company.

When the children finished their nap, their teachers took them back to Toyland to help the elves gather and package the Christmas presents for delivery. Tomorrow they would be leaving the North Pole and the following day was Christmas Eve. When Santa and his hay bale company finished their business, they strolled over to check on Little Toot and prepare him for departure the next morning. Santa crawled up in Little Toot's cab. He had never been in a train before. He double checked the flying powder as he smiled to himself. He found there was enough to get his little friend safely home with the children. He placed a Global Position System, GPS, in the cab to get Toot headed home in the right direction since at the North Pole the only direction is south.

When Gramps was satisfied that Little Toot was ready for the trip home, Ken and he went to Toyland with Santa. Santa had to double check his list he must deliver. They spent the rest of the afternoon checking the list and making sure the presents were ready to be delivered. Toyland was buzzing with the Christmas rush. The children were a great help and enjoyed working with the elf children. They all sang Christmas carols as they worked together. The teachers had been practicing with the children for the program they would perform for Santa and Mrs. Claus tonight in the barn. The children enjoyed singing and were anxious to entertain the elves, Santa and Mrs. Claus tonight.

When the evening meal was over in the community center,

everyone went to the barn for the children's program. The children sang at the top of their lungs. Before the program was finished, all the elf children had joined in the caroling. Santa even had to get up and sing. They had a festive time and even Wayne, the Christmas tree elf, joined in from his perch on the Christmas tree Gramps had borrowed from the school Christmas program and brought along to the North Pole. The old cowboy elf was sitting back in the corner by old Paint listening. He had never heard music like that ever before in his ears. All of the reindeer watched from their warm stalls. They would hear the children carol all around the world in two more days as they pulled the sleigh full of presents. It was bedtime for everyone when the program came to an end. Santa and Mrs. Claus hugged the teachers and each and every student as they thanked them for an entertaining evening.

Everyone gathered for breakfast the next morning at the North Pole community center. The elf ladies had prepared a hearty breakfast for all. Mrs. Middleton sat at the head table with Santa and Mrs. Claus. After all were seated, Mrs. Middleton stood up and thanked them for being great host and for inviting all of them for the visit. Santa then asked all to bow their head as he blessed the meal. When he finished all the adults said.

"Amen."

The room was buzzing with the sounds of excitement of the children. They had all enjoyed their visit but they were also anxious to see their families and join in the Christmas spirit at home. Everyone ate a hearty and healthy breakfast. It goes without saying Santa enjoyed every bite and his beard showed it. After the meal was finished the students stood up and sang, "We wish you a Merry Christmas," to Santa, Mrs. Claus, and all the elves. The teachers then helped them pack their belonging for the trip home. When they were all packed, they took the children with their belongings to Santa's house. Santa visited with the children and told them stories as their teachers finished packing their belongings. When all were packed they carried their luggage with the help of the elves to the shed where Little Toot was huffing and puffing as he waited for his precious cargo. Gramps and Ken loaded the baggage car under the watchful eye of Mrs. Middleton. When all the belongings were loaded, it was time to bid the host good-by and climb aboard.

Santa and Mrs. Claus stood on the train platform and hugged everyone as they prepared to climb the steps into Little Toot. When all were safely aboard, Santa motioned for Gramps to back Little Toot out of the shed. As Little Toot's engine reached where Santa and Mrs. Claus stood, he stopped for a moment as Gramps and Ken shook Santa's hand and gave Mrs. Claus a hug. Little Toot then gave out a puff of steam and a little toot as they backed out onto the runway. As Gramps opened Little Toot's throttle, the tiny wings extended on the side of the engine and cars. Smoke billowed out of Little Toot's stack into the air as he huffed and puffed down the runway gaining speed rapidly. After they lifted off, they circled back around for a final farewell toot to their friends waving below. Gramps noticed the smoke from Little Toot's stack was drifting over the white landscape where Santa stood with Mrs. Claus and the elves. As they were climbing out to their cruise altitude, Ken checked the GPS Santa had installed and set Little Toot on the correct heading for home and the children's anxiously awaiting parents.

Santa stood with his head elf, Rufus, and watched Little Toot leave a trail of coal smoke pollution as they climbed to reach their cruising altitude. He said to Rufus.

"Have the workers in Toyland pack the little toy diesel train I have been saving for a special gift. I am going to give it to Gramps this Christmas to replace Little Toot under his Christmas tree. Little Toot has just made his final Christmas trip. He is polluting our landscape and air."

LET THEM BE A CHILD

Santa thought of the children,
and the burden some must bear.
Just because their parents,
of them will not take care.

He looked up to the heavens,
and a star shining bright.
He thought of the Christ Child,
who was born this Holy night.

He knelt in his sleigh,
as he flew into the night.
He asked to find these children,
and make their burden light.

Take the burden they carry,
and on their parents it be piled.
Give them hope and love,
and let them be a child.

THE PAPER ANGEL

JOAN was sitting at her desk coloring a picture on a paper her kindergarten teacher had passed out. She had been instructed to color the little Christmas tree and then cut it out. When she finished she raised her hand to let her teacher know she was finished coloring and cutting the tree out. Her teacher checked her work and then handed her some papers with Christmas tree ornaments and other decorations drawn on them. On one paper was a little angel to be colored and cutout to glue on the top of her little tree.

Joan would bite her tongue as she worked ever so hard coloring ornaments and other Christmas tree decorations. The little angel really got her attention. She had been looking for a special angel for her grandma. She did not want to cut this angel out to glue on the tree top; she had other plans for it. She let her thoughts drift to a conversation she had with her grandpa one time. He had told her when he was not around to look after Grandma she would need a special angel to look after her. He had told his little granddaughter she would make a perfect angel for the job.

Grandpa had told her when he was gone he would be close by. He would be plowing on the back forty acres where shade trees grow along one side of it near a clear stream. She had walked with him under the shade trees and fished in the small stream. He had shown her where a cool clear spring bubbles up from the ground and feeds the stream. Grandpa always liked to farm the forty acres because when he was tired and his clothes soaked with sweat, he could rest in the shade of the trees and cool off as a soft breeze would blow. He called this Mother Nature's air conditioner.

Grandpa did go away and search as she may, she could never find him plowing the field or resting under the shade trees. The only place she could find him was in her memories. Her thoughts returned to the classroom. She would just ask her teacher if she could have an extra paper to color for a special Christmas present for her grandma. She raised her little hand and when her teacher called on her she said.

"I need to ask you a question."

Her teacher motioned for her to come over to her desk. Little Joan got up from her desk and walked over to her teacher. She placed her little hand up by her mouth so the other students could not see or hear what she had to ask the teacher. She whispered.

"Can I have another paper with the angel on it? I need the Angel for my grandma. My grandpa told me to be an angel and look over Grandma when he is working on the back forty. I want to watch over her but how can I when I am at school or at my house? I thought I could make a paper angel and put on her refrigerator to watch over her all the time. I can help the paper angel watch over Grandma when I go visit her."

Joan's teacher smiled and gave her two sheets of paper with the angel drawn on then. She watched as Joan skipped back to her desk and started coloring in earnest. She sat on one leg and was fidgety as she colored. She kept inside the lines as she colored and colored the little angel where she shined from head to foot. When she was through she got out her little scissors and ever so carefully cut the little angel out. When she was through her teacher looked at Joan's work. She was amazed to see the coloring and the way she had cut it out. The angel radiated with light from the colors. She had never seen Joan do this good of work before. Maybe this was a special angel Joan had made. She put a magnet on the back of the angel so Joan could hang it on her grandma's refrigerator door.

When Joan got off the bus after school, she ran straight to her room and took the little angel out of her backpack. She put her on her dresser ever so careful. She was anxious for the week end to get here so she could go visit Grandma and put the angel on her refrigerator. After she saw the angel had made it home safely from school, she was ready for a peanut butter and jelly sandwich in the kitchen along with a glass of milk. After she had eaten her snack she went back to her bedroom to check on the little paper angel and change into her play clothes.

She spent the rest of the afternoon playing in the backyard with her dog Wag. He was always glad to see her and would check to see if she had part of a sandwich left. Joan had made sure to save him a small piece. She had named him Wag because he was a happy dog and could not wag his tail without wagging his whole body. She told Wag all about the little angel she had colored and cut out at school to watch over her grandma. As she was talking to Wag, an idea formed in her mind. She would ask her mother if Wag could go with them when they went to the farm to visit Grandma. She would take Wag with her to the back forty to help her find Grandpa. Since she had an extra paper with an angel on it, she would color it tonight and cut it out for her grandpa.

The weekend finally arrived and the family along with Wag rode in the car to Grandma's house. Wag rode all the way with his head stuck out of the window smelling the fresh air and letting his ears flap in the wind. Grandma was standing on her front porch wiping her hands on her apron as they pulled in the driveway. Joan and Wag were the first out of the car. Grandma picked her granddaughter up and smothered her with kisses as Wag wagged around them. Her dad unloaded the light suitcases. They would be staying just for one night.

Joan always slept with her grandma in her big soft bed. She carried her overnight case into Grandma's bedroom and ever so carefully took the little angel out she had made for Grandma. She carried it into the kitchen to put on the refrigerator door. Her Grandma watched as Joan ever so gently placed the angel on the door. Joan said.

"Remember now, you and I have to watch over Grandma for Grandpa."

After lunch, Joan asked her dad to walk with Wag and her to the back forty. She had something special to hang on the shade tree where Grandpa always rested while Wag searched for Grandpa.

THE COMMUNITY HOUND

A young farm couple decided they wanted a dog on their farm. They knew where a litter of pups were, and decided to go look at them to see if they could purchase one. When they arrived they found a litter of six puppies aggravating their mother. They would not give her any rest at all. The puppies, they were told, are part Saint Bernard and the other part is country dog. One pup in particular caught their eye. It had sleepy eyes, long ears, big feet, and an outgoing personality about it. When they asked how much they wanted for the puppy that has caught their attention. They were told, "You can have whatever puppy you want. They are just half breeds. We will be glad to get rid of them."

The young couple picked the pup up with the sleepy eyes and outgoing personality, which had caught their eye. They thanked the people for the pup and took him to his new home. The pup had an appetite that matched his feet. It could be readily seen the pup would grow into a very large dog. He was always bouncing around the yard and chewing on everything in sight. He definitely was not a picky eater. If it was in his dog dish he made it disappear quicker than the time it took to dump it in his dish.

It just so happened, the young couple got along better with the pup than they got along with each other. When the pup was nine months old he watched them move everything out of the house and drive off separately. His food dish was soon empty and his water bowl was dry. They had left the small farm and abandoned him. He waited two days for them to return; he was thirsty and hungry. Thirst and hunger drove him to dig under the yard fence and to search the neighborhood. He soon found out the neighbors overall were all good farm folks. Some of the farmers at first were mean to him and tried to run him off when he ventured onto their property. He soon won them over with his easy going and friendly ways. After a while, everywhere he went, he found out the people would offer him something to eat and water to drink.

He would return to the abandoned farm house every night hoping to find the people had returned, but to no avail. Every morning he would start his routine of visiting the neighborhood looking for a hand out. He was always fed and met a lot of new dogs and their owners. He was a very likeable hound and never ever caused a moment of trouble. He never tried to fight another dog over a meal but found out they were usually willing to share. No one knew his name and his visits were short everyday. The people all just referred to him as the community hound. He would not let anyone adopt him, but they could feed and pet him all they wanted.

The folks in this community were musical and would all meet at a house on the corner of a cross road. Every Thursday evening they would bring their instruments and play. Some had banjos, guitars, fiddles, harmonicas, or any other musical instrument to their likings. The community hound was always among the first guests to arrive, rain or shine, to listen to the music. The musicians soon saw how much he liked music and named him Beethoven. As Beethoven listened to the music, his tail appeared to keep beat with it. After the music stopped every Thursday night, he would disappear into the night.

Beethoven would be seen every morning as he made his rounds, trotting along with the dogs where he had made his visits. It appeared they had it planned to all get together and then disappear into the woods for a day of hunting. They were all buddies and never fought over a single thing. Beethoven towered over all the rest of his friends, but he only appeared to be their leader when they were gathering in the morning and when they went home in the evening. After a day of hunting, they would be seen trotting down the road and as they passed by each dog's home it would drop out. By the time Beethoven arrived at his vacant farm home, he was alone. The next morning Beethoven would make his rounds for any handouts he could get and collect his friends. They all soon became a familiar sight. It was kind of humorous to people who saw them because they were all different sizes. The only thing they had in common was they were all mix breed or yard dogs as some folks call them. One little dog had to take five steps to Beethoven's one. He could run under his large friend and never touch him.

Sometimes when the men were riding their four wheeled vehicles to check on their crops or maybe the fencing, Beethoven would suddenly appear out of no where and run along side of them. The first time this would happen, it would kind of intimidate the rider. Beethoven stood as tall as the handlebars on the four wheelers and liked to run along side and race them. They soon found out there was not one mean bone in Beethoven body. Beethoven kept a regular schedule in the morning but during the day if he was not hunting in the woods with his friends, he could show up anywhere.

When the people in the community got together for a fund raiser Beethoven was always present to help by keeping the children occupied. He liked it best when the ladies cooked and sold meals for their fund raiser. He was always right there in line to get his dish of food. The ladies never disappointed him either. The children also saw to it Beethoven was well fed. Where ever there was a community gathering, Beethoven somehow knew about it and was among the first to arrive.

When the children went on a hay ride, there was Beethoven sitting on the hayrack enjoying it as much as the children. He liked all the children and made sure each and everyone received a love kiss by his big tongue. When the children went on a hayride and then set around a bonfire roasting wieners, Beethoven was there looking into the fire at the hotdogs roasting on a stick. He would drool all over. As usual, some hotdogs would be dropped by accident and on purpose, those hotdogs were for Beethoven. When he was on the hayrack riding with the children, he always sat right smack dab in the middle. If anyone ever saw the children and Beethoven on the hayride, they would have to smile. He would be sitting up proud as could be and enjoying every moment.

Beethoven would see that all the children in the community never missed their bus. He knew every nook and cranny in the woods and every short cut. He would take these shortcuts to see the children off to school in the morning and be there to meet them in the afternoon. Some of the children would have part of their lunch or snack in their backpack to share with him. He was very protective of them. Try as the children may, not a one of them could make Beethoven be their very own dog and stay in their yard.

Beethoven never held a grudge, although he could have for being abandoned and made to survive on his own. He was and still is an inspiration to the families who live in the farm community. They always watched for him and if for any reason he would not show up at their house for a meal, they would go looking for him. He has personality plus and it makes the people in the community realize you can forgive and be happy. Beethoven lives one day at a time and accepts life as it has been given him. He appears to see the sunshine every day even if the sun is behind some clouds.